Amy's brown eyes were anxious, despite the calm she appeared to radiate.

'Here. My turn to cuddle Hope and keep her happy for a bit,' Josh said.

And that was definitely gratitude in her eyes as she handed the baby over.

Though her hands brushed against his as they transferred the baby between them, and a frisson of desire flickered down his spine.

Inappropriate. Amy was his neighbour, and he was helping out with a tricky situation. That was it, he reminded himself. He wasn't going to hit on her and he wasn't going to let himself wonder how soft her hair was, or how her skin would feel against his.

'Can I get you a drink?' she asked.

'A glass of wine would be lovely right now,' he admitted.

And it might distract him from all the ridiculous thoughts flickering through his head. Thoughts about how Amy's mouth was a perfect Cupid's bow, and wondering what it would feel like if he kissed her.

Dear Reader,

I love writing friends-to-lovers books—or, in this case, acquaintances-to-lovers. I also have a bit of a weakness for babies—especially at Christmas. Hence Amy and Josh, who are both really not looking forward to Christmas, find a baby on their doorstep… And Hope—the baby—changes absolutely everything.

I have to admit to borrowing a few things here. A baby rushed to hospital at Christmas… That's my youngest—though she was six weeks rather than two days old. A baby weighing 5lbs 10oz… That's my cousin's daughter when I met her at a week old—while I was writing this book, actually, though the book was planned well before Sofia-Grace arrived! And the burning food… That's where my husband takes a bow. And that's also why I do all the cooking in our house!

I hope you enjoy Amy and Josh's story. And I wish you all the very best of the holiday season.

With love,

Kate Hardy X

HER FESTIVE DOORSTEP BABY

BY
KATE HARDY

Published in Great Britain 2016
By Mills & Boon, an imprint of HarperCollins*Publishers*
1 London Bridge Street, London, SE1 9GF

© 2016 Pamela Brooks

ISBN: 978-0-263-06589-3

Our policy is to use papers that are natural, renewable and recyclable
products and made from wood grown in sustainable forests. The logging
and manufacturing processes conform to the legal environmental
regulations of the country of origin.

Printed and bound in Great Britain
by CPI Antony Rowe, Chippenham, Wiltshire

RF

Kate Hardy has always loved books and could read before she went to school. She discovered Mills & Boon books when she was twelve and decided this was what she wanted to do. When she isn't writing Kate enjoys reading, cinema, ballroom dancing and the gym. You can contact her via her website: katehardy.com.

Books by Kate Hardy

Mills & Boon Romance

Falling for the Secret Millionaire
Behind the Film Star's Smile
Crown Prince, Pregnant Bride
A New Year Marriage Proposal
It Started at a Wedding...
Falling for Mr December
Billionaire, Boss...Bridegroom?

Visit the Author Profile page at millsandboon.co.uk for more titles.

For Sofia-Grace, the newest baby in our family—
with lots of love on your first Christmas. xxx

CHAPTER ONE

Friday 24th December

'HELLO? HELLO?'

There was no answer. It was probably a courier in the middle of a super-frantic shift, Amy thought, needing to deliver as many parcels as humanly possible on Christmas Eve and pressing every single button on the intercom in the hope of finding someone who'd buzz the front door open so they could leave a parcel in the lobby. The silence probably meant they'd stopped waiting for her to answer and were already trying someone else.

She was about to replace the receiver on her intercom system when she heard a noise.

It sounded like a baby crying.

Was it her imagination? Or maybe the courier was listening to something on the radio. An ad, perhaps.

She knew that she was being ridiculous, but something made Amy go out of her own front door and into the main lobby, just to check that everything was all right.

And there, in the corner by the front door, was a cardboard box.

Except she could still hear a baby crying, and this time she was pretty sure it wasn't on a radio.

When she drew closer, she could see that the cardboard box wasn't a parcel at all. The top of the box was open. Inside, wrapped in a soft blanket, was a baby. There were traces of blood on the baby's face and Amy had a moment of panic; but then she thought that the blood might be because the baby was very, very young.

Young enough to be a newborn.

Who on earth would leave a newborn baby in a cardboard box, in the lobby of a block of flats?

She quickly opened the front door and looked outside, but there wasn't anyone in the street who looked as if they'd just left a baby on a doorstep. Nobody running away or huddled in a hoodie, trying to hide their face.

What were you supposed to do when you found an abandoned baby? Should she take the baby straight to hospital to be checked over, or should she ring the police? If she moved the box or picked the baby up to try to soothe it, would she be disturbing forensic evidence that would help the police find the baby's mother?

Yet the baby was so tiny, and the lobby wasn't heated. She could hardly leave the poor little mite to freeze there. She was about to try the other intercoms to see if any of her neighbours was in and could ring the police for her, when the door to the lobby opened and Josh Farnham walked in.

She didn't know Josh very well; he'd moved into one of the flats on her floor about six months ago. They were on smile-and-nod terms, and she occasionally took in a parcel for him, but that was about it.

'Is everything OK?' he asked. And then he frowned as the baby cried again.

'No.' Amy gestured to the cardboard box. 'Someone's just left a baby on our doorstep.'

Josh looked utterly shocked. 'A *baby*? But—who?'

'I have no idea.'

He bent down to touch the baby's hand. Clearly he had the magic touch because the baby immediately stopped crying.

'Someone pressed my intercom but didn't speak,' Amy continued. 'I assumed it was a courier trying to find someone in so they could deliver a parcel to someone in our block, but then I thought I could hear a baby crying.' She spread her hands. 'It could've been on the radio, but something made me come out here to see, just in case. That's when I found the baby.' She bit her lip. 'There's blood on the baby's face, but I think that might be because the baby's a newborn. As in *really* newborn.'

'Have you called the police?' he asked, his blue eyes narrowing.

'I was just about to,' she said, 'but I didn't bring my phone out with me, and I'm not sure if I'm going to mess up the forensics or what have you if I take the baby into my flat.'

'You can hardly wait out here until the police arrive,' Josh said, frowning. 'Both of you would freeze. Look, let me grab some stuff from my flat so I can put up a makeshift barrier round the area where the box is now, to protect any potential evidence, then I'll check the baby over properly while you call the police.' The concern clearly showed in her expression, because he added, 'It's OK. I'm qualified. I'm a doctor in the local emergency department.'

That would explain why she hardly ever saw him. His shifts at the hospital would be very different from her own hours teaching at the local high school. But most of all Amy felt relief that she wasn't going to have to deal with this completely on her own. Where babies were concerned, she was totally clueless, and Josh seemed to know how to deal with them. 'All right. Thanks,' she said.

'I'll be quick,' he promised.

'Should I pick the baby up?' she asked when the crying started again.

'Movement usually helps settle a crying baby. If you walk up and down—obviously avoiding the area where whoever left the baby might've trodden—the baby will probably stop crying.'

That sounded like experience talking. Better and better: because Amy was very used to dealing with teenagers, but her dealings with babies had been minimal.

Especially since Michael had ended their engagement.

She pushed the thought away. *Not now.* She needed to concentrate on helping this abandoned baby, not brood over the wreckage of her past.

'What about supporting the baby's head?' she asked.

'Just hold the baby against you, like this,' Josh said, picking the baby out of the box and then holding the baby close to him to demonstrate, with one hand cradled round the baby's head so it didn't flop back.

'OK.' Carefully, Amy took the baby from him.

His hands brushed briefly against hers and it felt as if she'd been galvanised.

Oh, for pity's sake. Yes, the man was pretty—despite the fact that he needed a shave and she suspected that he'd dragged his fingers rather than a comb through his wavy dark hair—but for all she knew he could be in a serious relationship. This was so inappropriate. Even if he wasn't in a relationship, she didn't want to get involved with anyone. Because then eventually she'd have to admit to her past, and he'd walk away from her—just as Michael had. And then that would make their relationship as neighbours awkward. Amy knew she was better off on her own and keeping all her relationships platonic. Josh Farnham might be one of the most attractive men she'd ever met, but he wasn't for her.

Hoping that he'd mistake her flustered state for nerves about dealing with the baby—which was partially true in any case—Amy murmured something anodyne and started walking up and down the lobby with the baby.

Josh came back what felt like hours later but could only have been five minutes, carrying several tin cans, a pile of bandages, safety pins, a marker pen and a spiral-bound notebook.

'Are you OK to keep holding the baby?' he asked.

No. It was bringing back all kinds of emotions that Amy would much rather suppress. But she wasn't going to burden a near-stranger with her private misery. 'Sure,' she fibbed.

Josh swiftly wrote out some notes saying, *Please do not touch—waiting for police*, then marked off the area where Amy had found the cardboard box. When he'd finished, he held out his arms for the baby. 'My turn, I think,' he said.

'Thanks,' she said, grateful to be relieved of her burden. Though again her hands touched his as they transferred the baby between them, and again she felt that peculiar and inappropriate response to him, that flare of desire. She picked up the box. 'I'd better bring this.'

He nodded. 'Your flat or mine?'

'Mine, I guess,' she said.

She let them into her flat, then called the police and explained what had happened while Josh examined the baby. She couldn't help watching him while she was talking; he was so gentle and yet so sure at the same time. He checked the baby over thoroughly before wrapping the infant in the soft blanket again.

The baby wasn't wearing a nappy and had no clothes. They definitely had a problem here. And what would happen once the baby got hungry? Amy had absolutely nothing in her kitchen that was suitable for a newborn, let alone any way of feeding a baby.

'The police are on their way now. They said they'll contact Social Services and meet them here, too,' she said when she put the phone down. 'How's the baby?'

'Doing fine,' Josh said. 'Our doorstep baby's a little girl. Definitely a newborn. But I'd say she's a couple of weeks early and I'm a bit worried about the mum. She clamped the umbilical cord with one of those clips you use on packaging to keep things fresh, and my guess is she's very young and didn't tell anyone she was having the baby, and she didn't go to hospital so she had the birth somewhere on her own.'

'And then she put the baby in a box and left her in our lobby with no clothes, no nappy, no milk—just the blanket,' Amy said. She winced. 'The poor girl must've really been desperate. Do you see that kind of thing a lot at the hospital?'

'Abandoned babies, improvised cord clamps or complete lack of any baby things?' he asked. 'Not very often to any of them, let alone all three together. Though on the rare occasions the police do bring in an abandoned baby, it usually turns out that the mum's very young and very scared.'

'The police might be able to find this baby's mum and get her to hospital so she can be checked over,' Amy said.

'Let's hope so,' Josh said, sounding very far from convinced.

'I'm sorry. I rather hijacked you when you came into the lobby,' she said. 'I guess now the police are on their way I ought to let you get on.'

Josh didn't know Amy Howes very well—just that she lived in one of the other flats on his floor and she'd taken in a parcel for him a couple of times. He had no idea what she did for a living or even if she had a job.

But what he did know was that her brown eyes were sad behind her smile, and she'd looked slightly panicky at the idea of being responsible for a baby, even for the short time it would take between now and the police arriving. Especially as the baby didn't even have the basics for any kind of care.

He'd only been going to pick up some milk and bread anyway. It wasn't important. The open-all-hours shop round the corner from the hospital would probably still be open when he'd finished his shift, even though it was Christmas Eve.

Not that you'd know it was Christmas, in Amy's flat. There were a couple of cards propped up on the mantelpiece, and a few more stacked in a pile, but there wasn't a tree or any presents. Even when people were going away for Christmas, they usually displayed their cards and had some kind of decorations up. Maybe she didn't celebrate Christmas. Was that because it was too painful for her—like it was for him?

Though it wasn't any of his business.

He shouldn't get involved.

He didn't want to get involved.

And yet he found his mouth opening and the wrong words coming out. 'I'm not due at the hospital until eleven, so I can stay with you until the police get here, if you like.'

'I can't impose on you like that,' she said.

Which was his get-out clause. He ought to agree with her and leave as fast as he could. Though his mouth definitely didn't seem to be with the programme. 'It's not that much of an imposition. If I'd left my flat a couple of minutes earlier, I would've been the one to find the baby,' he said. 'And my medical knowledge might be helpful to the police.'

'True,' she said, looking relieved and grateful. 'Thank you. I have to admit I was a bit worried about looking after the baby on my own.'

'Not used to babies?'

He couldn't quite read the expression on her face before she masked it, but he knew instantly that he'd put his foot in it. Right now he had a pretty good idea that whatever had caused the sadness behind her eyes had involved a baby. A miscarriage, perhaps? Or IVF that hadn't worked and her relationship hadn't survived the strain? And maybe Christmas was the anniversary of everything going wrong for her, just as it was for him?

Not that it was any of his business. And again he reminded himself not to get involved. That pull he felt towards Amy Howes was definitely something he shouldn't act on. If she was recovering from a broken heart, the last thing she needed was to get involved with someone whose track record at relationships was as poor as his.

'I'm more used to dealing with teens,' Amy said. 'I teach maths at the local high school.'

Now that he hadn't expected. 'You don't look like a maths teacher.'

She smiled, then, and Josh's heart felt as if it had turned over. Which was anatomically impossible in the first place; and in the second place Kelly's betrayal had put him off relationships for good. Back off, he reminded himself.

'I'm definitely better at explaining surds and synthetic division than I am at changing nappies,' she said. 'Though that's not the biggest problem. The baby's going to need some nappies and some clothes. I don't know anyone in our block or nearby with a baby who could lend us anything.'

'Me neither,' he said.

'Even if the police arrive in the next five minutes, they're going to be asking questions and what have you—and I have no idea how quickly the baby's going to need a nappy.'

'The average newborn goes through ten to fifteen a day,' Josh said.

'So basically every two to three hours. I could probably make a makeshift nappy out of a towel, but that's not fair on the poor baby.' She shook her head. 'The supermarket on the corner will sell nappies and they might sell some very basic baby clothes. Toss you for it?'

'I'll go,' Josh said. 'I needed to get some bread and milk anyway. I'll pick up nappies, some clothes and some formula milk.'

The panicky look was back on Amy's face. 'What if the baby starts crying again while you're gone?'

'Pick her up and cuddle her. If all else fails, sing to her,' Josh said. 'That usually works.'

'That sounds like experience talking.'

'I'm an uncle of three,' he said. Though he was guiltily aware that he hadn't seen much of his nieces and nephew since his divorce. His family's pity had been hard enough to take, but then he'd become very aware that most of his family saw him as a failure for letting his marriage go down the tubes—and he really couldn't handle that. It had been easier to use work as an excuse to avoid them. Which was precisely why he was working at the hospital over Christmas: it meant he didn't have to spend the holiday with his family and face that peculiar mixture of pity and contempt.

'Any songs in particular?' Amy asked.

'Anything,' he said. 'The baby won't care if you're not word-perfect; she just wants a bit of comfort. I'll see you in a few minutes.' He scribbled his mobile phone number on one of the spare pieces of paper from their makeshift 'crime scene' barrier. 'Here's my number.'

'Thanks. I'll text you in a minute so you've got my number. And I'd better give you some money for the baby stuff.'

'We'll sort it out between us later,' he said. 'Is there anything you need from the supermarket?'

'Thanks, but I did all my shopping yesterday,' she said.

If Josh had done that, too, instead of feeling that he was too tired to move after a hard shift, then he wouldn't have been walking through the lobby when Amy had found the baby, and he wouldn't have been involved with any of this. Though he instantly dismissed the thought as mean. It wasn't the baby's fault that she'd been abandoned, and it wasn't the baby's fault that caring for a baby, even for a few minutes, made it feel as if someone had ripped the top off his scars.

'See you in a bit,' he said, relieved to escape.

Amy looked at the sleeping baby.

A newborn.

Eighteen months ago, this was what she'd wanted most in the world. She and Michael had tried for a baby for a year without success, and they'd been at the point of desperation when they'd walked into the doctor's office after her scan.

And then they'd learned the horrible, horrible truth.

Even though Amy hadn't had a clue and it hadn't actually been her fault that her Fallopian tubes were damaged beyond repair, Michael had blamed her for it—and he'd walked out on her. She'd hoped that maybe once he'd had time to think about it, they could talk it through and get past the shock, but he hadn't been able to do that. All he could see was that Amy had given him an STD, and because of that STD she was infertile and couldn't give him a baby. He wouldn't even consider IVF, let alone adoption or fostering. Even though Amy hadn't had any symptoms, so she'd had no idea that her ex had given her chlamydia, Michael still blamed her for being too stupid to realise it for herself.

The injustice still rankled.

But it wasn't this baby's fault.

Or the fault of the baby's mum.

'Life,' she told the baby, 'is complicated.'

And then she wished she hadn't said a word when the baby started crying.

Pick her up and cuddle her—that was Josh's advice. Except it didn't work and the baby just kept crying.

He'd also suggested singing, as a last resort. But what did you sing to a baby? Every song Amy knew had gone out of her head.

It was Christmas. Sing a carol, she told herself.

'Silent Night' turned out to be a very forlorn hope indeed. It didn't encourage the baby to be quiet in the slightest. 'Hark the Herald Angels Sing' was more like 'Hark the Little Baby Screams'.

This was terrible. She really hoped Josh came back with supplies soon. There was bound to be a massive queue at the checkouts, and what if the supermarket had run out of nappies?

Maybe a Christmas pop song would help. She tried a couple of old classics, but the baby didn't seem to like them, either.

If only Josh had let her toss a coin. As a maths teacher, she knew the probability was fifty-fifty—but she also knew that actually there was a tiny, tiny weighting in favour of heads. She would've called heads and could've been the one to go out for supplies. And Josh, who seemed far better with babies than she was, would've been able to comfort this poor little girl much more easily than Amy could. And how could someone so tiny make so much noise?

'I can't do this,' she said, trying very hard not to burst into tears herself. 'I don't know how to make everything better, baby. I can't even fix my own life, so how can I possibly fix yours?'

The baby was still crying when there was a knock on her door. To her relief, it was Josh.

'Having trouble?' he asked on seeing the red-faced, screaming baby.

'Just a bit,' Amy said dryly. Though it wasn't fair to be sarcastic to him. It wasn't his fault that she was hopelessly inexperienced with babies. 'I tried singing to her. Let's just say she doesn't like Christmas carols. Or Christmas pop songs. And I'm out of ideas.'

'OK. Let me try.' He put the bag on the floor, took the baby from her and started singing 'All I Want for Christmas is You'.

Immediately, the baby stopped crying.

'Clearly you have the knack,' Amy said.

He laughed. 'Maybe she just likes the song.'

Or his voice. He had a gorgeous singing voice, rich and deep. The kind of voice that made your knees feel as if they were melting. To cover her confusion, she asked, 'How did you get on at the supermarket?'

'Ready-mixed formula milk, a couple of bottles, a pack of newborn nappies, some baby bath stuff, three vests and three sleep suits,' he said, indicating the bag. 'Oh, and my milk and bread.'

'Do you want to put the milk in my fridge for now?' she asked.

'Thanks. That'd be good.' Then he grimaced. 'Um.

I think we're going to have to give her a bath sooner rather than later.'

Amy could see the wet patch spreading on the blanket. 'And wash that blanket?'

'Maybe leave the blanket until the police say it's OK to wash it, but we can't leave the baby wet. Is it OK to use your bathroom to clean her up?'

'Sure. I've got plenty of towels.' She found the softest ones in the airing cupboard and placed one on the radiator to keep it warm while Josh ran water into the bath. This felt oddly domestic: and it was almost exactly as she'd imagined her life being with Michael and their baby.

Except, thanks to Gavin, she couldn't have babies. And Michael was no longer part of her life. She'd heard that he'd got married and had a baby on the way, so he'd managed to make his dreams come true—because Amy was no longer holding him back.

She shook herself. This thing with the abandoned baby was only temporary. As soon as the police had taken a statement from her and from Josh, they'd take the baby to some kind of foster home and she probably wouldn't see Josh again for weeks. That frisson of desire she'd felt when his skin had brushed against hers was utterly ridiculous, and she needed to be sensible about this instead of moping for something she couldn't have.

Josh tested the temperature of the water with his elbow. 'OK. Time for your first bath, little one.'

At the first touch of the water, the baby screamed the place down. Even Josh looked fraught by the time he'd finished bathing her, and Amy's teeth were on edge.

The screams abated to grizzling once the baby was out of the bath and wrapped in the warm towel.

'She's hungry, probably,' Josh said.

Amy's heart contracted sharply. 'Poor little mite.' And how desperate the baby's mother must've been to abandon her.

Between them they managed to get the baby into the nappy and sleep suit, and Josh rocked the baby and crooned softly to her while Amy sterilised one of the bottles he'd bought and warmed the formula milk in a jug of hot water. And then it was her turn to cuddle the baby and feed her.

Sitting there, with the baby cradled on her lap, watching her drink greedily from the bottle of milk, really tugged at Amy's heart.

If she'd been less clueless about Gavin's real character—or, better still, hadn't dated him in the first place—her life could have been so different. She could've been sitting here cuddling her own baby, next to the man of her dreams. Instead, here she was, desperately trying to fill her life with work, and right now she was holding a baby she'd have to give back.

She couldn't help glancing at Josh. His expression was unreadable but, before he masked it, she saw definite pain in his eyes. He'd said that he was an uncle of three, but she had a feeling there was a bit more to it than that.

Had he lost a child?

Had someone broken his heart?

Not that it was any of her business. He was her neighbour. They knew next to nothing about each other. And that was the way things were in London. You avoided eye contact as much as you could, smiled and nodded politely if you couldn't avoid eye contact, and you most definitely didn't get involved.

The baby fell asleep almost the second after she'd finished her feed. Amy folded up a towel as a make-shift bed and placed the baby on it, covering her with another towel. She'd just tucked the baby in when her intercom buzzed.

Thankfully the noise didn't wake the baby. 'Hello?'

'It's the police. PC Graham and PC Walters.'

She buzzed them in.

One of them was carrying a sturdy metal case, which she presumed contained forensic equipment, and the other had a notebook.

'I like the scene-of-crime tape improvisation in the lobby,' the first policeman said with a smile. 'I assume you'd like the bandages back when I've finished?'

Josh smiled back. 'No. It's fine to get rid of them. Do you think you'll get anything to help you track down the baby's mother?'

'I'll go and dust the area now,' the first police-man said, 'while my colleague PC Graham here goes through everything with you.'

'Shall I put the kettle on?' Amy asked.

'That'd be lovely. Thank you,' PC Walters said, heading out of the door with his case.

'Mr and Mrs Howes, isn't it?' PC Graham asked.

'Ms Howes and Mr Farnham,' she corrected. 'We're neighbours.'

'I see.' He made a note. 'Would you mind taking me through what happened?'

Between them, Amy and Josh filled in all the de-tails of how they'd found the baby.

'I'm a doctor,' Josh said. 'I've checked the baby

over, and she's fine. I think from all the vernix on her face—that's the white stuff—she's a couple of weeks early, and I have a feeling the mum might be quite young. I'd be a lot happier if you could find the mum and get her checked over, too, because she's at a high risk of infection.'

'It might take a while to find her,' PC Graham said.

'I'm afraid we had to give the baby a bath,' Amy added. 'She didn't have a nappy or any clothes, just the blanket, and the blanket got a bit, um, messy. I haven't washed it yet, in case you need it for forensics, but I've put it in a plastic bag.'

'Thank you. So you didn't recognise the voice over the intercom?' PC Graham asked.

'Nobody spoke,' Amy said. 'I just assumed it was a courier. Then I heard what sounded like a baby's cry. I don't know why, but some instinct made me go out and see for myself.'

'Just as well you did,' the policeman said. 'And you don't know anyone who might have left the baby here?'

'I don't know anyone who's pregnant,' Amy said. Mainly because she'd distanced herself from all her friends and colleagues who'd been trying for a baby, once she'd found out that she could no longer have children herself. It had been too painful being reminded of what she'd lost.

'So what happens now?' Josh asked.

'Once the social worker's here, she'll take the baby to the hospital,' the policeman said.

Josh shook his head. 'I don't really think that's a good idea. Right now, the children's ward is stuffed full of little ones with bronchiolitis.'

'Bronchi-what?' PC Graham asked.

'Bronchiolitis. It's a virus,' Josh explained. 'If adults catch it they get a really stinking cold, but in babies the mucus gums up the tiny airways in the lungs—the bronchioles—and they can't breathe or feed properly. Usually they end up being on oxygen therapy and being tube-fed for a week. And I really wouldn't want a newborn catching it—at that age it's likely to be really serious.'

'What about the general ward?' PC Graham asked. 'Could they look after her there?'

Josh shook his head. 'At this time of year the winter vomiting virus and flu are both doing the rounds in all the wards. As a newborn, she's at high risk of picking up either or both.'

The policeman shrugged and spread his hands. 'Then I don't know. We'll see what the social worker says when she gets here.'

By the time Amy had made mugs of tea, PC Walters was back from his forensic examination of the hallway.

'Did you manage to get anything?' Amy asked.

'A smudged footprint, but no fingerprints. Hopefully we'll get something from the box she left the baby in.' PC Walters looked at Amy's pale beige carpet. 'Though I'm afraid fingerprint powder's a bit messy.'

'It doesn't matter. It won't take that long to vacuum it up afterwards,' Amy said. 'It's more important that you discover something that'll help you find the baby's mum.'

But he didn't manage to get much from the box, either. 'There's a couple of long blonde hairs, but they don't necessarily belong to the mother. Though I found an envelope under the newspaper at the bottom of the box.'

'Newspaper?' Josh asked.

'For insulation against the cold, maybe,' PC Walters said. 'There's a gold chain in there and a note—though there aren't any prints. There are a couple of fibres, so she was probably wearing gloves.'

Amy read the note and then passed it to Josh.

Please look after Hope. I'm sorry.

'So the baby's name is Hope?' Josh asked.

'Seems so.'

Amy shared a glance with Josh. *Hope.* How terribly sad, because hope was clearly the last thing the baby's mother felt right now.

'Do you recognise the handwriting at all?' PC Graham asked.

'No,' Amy said.

'Me neither,' Josh agreed.

'We can take the box back with us—and the blanket—but I don't think it's going to help much,' PC Walters said, accepting a mug of tea.

They went through the whole lot again when Jane Richards, the social worker, arrived ten minutes later.

'So what's going to happen to the baby?' Amy asked.

Jane grimaced. 'At this time of year, everyone's on leave. You're lucky if you can get anyone even to answer a phone. And with Christmas falling partly on a weekend, the chances of getting hold of someone who can offer a foster care placement are practically zero. So I guess the baby's going to have to stay in hospital for a while.'

'The local hospital's on black alert,' Josh said.

'Apart from the fact that beds are in really short supply right now, there's bronchiolitis on the children's ward, and there's flu and the winter vomiting virus in the rest of the hospital. The chances are that Hope would go down with something nasty, so they'll refuse to take her.'

Jane looked at Amy. 'As you're the one who found her, and Christmas is meant to be the season of goodwill... Would you be able to look after her for a few days?'

'Me?' Amy looked at her in shock. 'But don't you have to do all kinds of background checks on me, first?'

'You're a teacher,' Jane said, 'so you'll already have gone through most of the checks. The rest of it is just formalities and, as I'm the senior social worker on duty in this area today, I can use my discretion.'

'I'm more used to dealing with teenagers,' Amy said. 'I've not really had much to do with babies.' Much less the baby she'd so desperately wanted to have with Michael. Something that could never, ever happen for her. 'I'm not sure...' And yet Jane was right. Christmas was the season of goodwill. How could Amy possibly turn away a helpless, defenceless newborn baby?

'I could help out,' Josh said. 'I'm working today and tomorrow, but I could help out between my shifts.'

So she'd have someone to talk things over with, if she was concerned. Someone who had experience of babies—and, better still, was a doctor.

But there was one possible sticking point. Even though she knew it was intrusive, she still had to ask. 'Will your partner mind?' she asked.

'I don't have a partner,' Josh said, and for a moment she saw a flash of pain in his expression.

Did he, too, have an ex who'd let him down badly? Amy wondered. She was pretty sure that, like her, he lived alone.

'I can make decisions without having to check with anyone first,' he said. 'How about yours?'

'Same as you,' she said.

'Which makes it easy.' He turned to Jane. 'OK. We'll look after Hope between us. How long do you need us to look after her?'

She winced. 'Until New Year's Eve, maybe?'

A whole week? 'Just as well it's the school holidays,' Amy said wryly.

'I'm off for a couple of days between Christmas and New Year,' Josh said. 'I'll do as much as I can. But the baby has nothing, Jane. I just went out to get emergency milk, nappies and enough clothes to keep her going until you got here. Her mother left her wrapped in a blanket in the box, and there wasn't anything with her. Well, the police found a note and a gold chain that the mum obviously wanted the baby to have,' he amended, 'but the baby doesn't have any clothes.'

'We don't have anywhere for her to sleep—and, apart from the fact that the police have taken the box, a cardboard box really isn't a suitable bed for a baby,' Amy added.

'I can help there,' Jane said. 'We have things in the office. I can bring you a Moses basket, bedding, nappies and spare clothes, and I can organise milk. Do you have any bottles?'

'Two,' Josh said, 'and I bought a couple of cartons

of ready-mixed formula. We've muddled through with very hot water to sterilise them for now.'

'If you don't mind mixing up your own formula, I can organise more bottles and sterilising equipment,' Jane said. 'What about the baby's mum?'

'We haven't got much on the forensics side,' PC Walters said. 'The best we can do is to put out a press release and ask the local media to tell her to get in touch.'

'If she's as young as I think she might be,' Josh said, 'she'll be worried that she's in trouble—especially if she managed to hide her pregnancy.'

'Strictly speaking, it's a criminal offence to abandon a baby,' PC Graham said, 'but judges are always lenient in the case of newborns and very young, very frightened mums.'

'She really needs to get to hospital or a doctor and let them check her over,' Josh said. 'That's important because, if she's retained any of the placenta or she tore during the delivery, there's a high risk she'll develop an infection—and if it's left untreated she could become really ill.'

'We'll make sure everyone says she won't be in any trouble and we're worried about her health,' PC Graham said.

'And tell her the baby's absolutely fine and being looked after. The poor girl's probably going to be worrying about that, too,' Amy added.

Josh looked at his watch. 'Sorry. I'm going to have to leave you now. I need to be at work.' He scribbled a number on one of the spare sheets of paper. 'You've got my mobile number, Amy, and this is my direct line in the department. You can get a message to me if it's urgent. I'll be back about half-past eight this evening—unless there's a crisis in the department, in which case I'll get a message to you as early as I can.'

Amy really hoped that she wasn't going to have to use that number. 'OK. Thanks.' She paused, knowing that this probably sounded like a come-on, but hoping that he'd take it as the practical suggestion it actually was. 'Look, as you're helping me with the baby, you might as well have dinner here. It's as easy to cook for two as for one.'

'That'd be nice.'

They exchanged a glance, and another frisson of desire ran down her spine—which was completely inappropriate. OK, so they were both single, but this was all about caring for Hope, not having a wild fling with her neighbour.

She fought to keep herself sounding professional. 'Do you have any food allergies, or is there anything you don't eat?'

'No to the allergies.' He smiled. 'As for the rest, I'm a medic in the emergency department, so we tend not to be fussy. We're lucky if we get a chance to grab a chocolate bar. As long as it's food and it's hot, I'm happy.'

She smiled back. 'OK.'

Once Josh had left, PC Graham sorted out the last bits of paperwork and the police left, too.

'I'll be back later this afternoon with supplies,' Jane promised.

'We should have enough milk and nappies to last until then,' Amy said.

'Thanks.' Jane smiled at her. 'You're a life-saver—literally.'

'Not just me. My neighbour helped.' And Amy really had to remind herself that Josh was just her neighbour. They might know each other a bit better and be on friendlier terms after the next few days, but this would be a platonic relationship only.

Amy saw Jane out of the flat, then returned to watch Hope sleeping in her makeshift bed. 'It looks as if it's just you and me, baby,' she said softly. 'For the next week you're going to have complete strangers looking after you and trying to make a family for you.'

But it was Christmas, the season of miracles. With any luck Hope's mum would come forward, Jane would be able to help her, and there would be a happy ending.

CHAPTER TWO

It was Hope's first Christmas, but Amy's flat looked just like it did on every other day of the year. She hadn't planned to be here for the festive season, so she hadn't bothered putting up a tree. When her plans had fallen through, it had felt like too much effort to get the Christmas decorations out. What was the point when she'd be here on her own?

Now, she had a reason to change that.

Even though she knew the baby wouldn't remember it or even have a clue that it was Christmas, Amy wanted to decorate her flat and make it Christmassy for Hope. Though, between feeds and nappy changes and cuddles to stop the baby crying, it took her four times as long as she'd expected. And she was panicking that she wasn't looking after Hope properly.

'I really have no idea what I'm doing,' she informed the baby, who cried a little bit more, as if agreeing with Amy. 'And I don't know who to ask. If I call Mum, she'll worry and get the next plane home from Canada—and that's not fair, because it's my parents' turn to spend Christmas with my brother Scott and his wife Rae.' Who didn't have children yet, so she couldn't ask her brother or sister-in-law for advice, either. 'Half my colleagues have teenagers, and I'm guessing they're way past remembering what the first couple of days with a newborn are like. And I'm a total cow because I distanced myself from my friends who do have babies. I can hardly ring them and ask for help when I've been so horrible and ignored their babies.'

But it had been too raw, once she'd learned that she was infertile and her dreams of having a baby were never coming true. Although she'd been genuinely pleased for her friends, she just hadn't been able to face watching them bloom through pregnancy or listening to them talk about the latest milestone their babies had reached.

But now she had a baby.

Temporarily.

And walking up and down with Hope like this, holding her close and rocking her in the hope that it would help settle her and stop her crying... This was what Amy's life could've been like, had it not been for Gavin and her own naivety. Why hadn't she even considered that, as he'd been serially unfaithful to her, in the process he might have picked up some kind of STD which didn't have any symptoms and passed it on to her? Why hadn't she got herself checked out just as a precautionary measure?

Maybe because she wasn't the suspicious sort— which was why it had taken her months in the first place to work out that Gavin was seeing other women on the side. A whole string of them. And she'd been stupidly oblivious, thinking everything was just fine between them.

'I'm an idiot,' she said with a sigh. 'But I'll do my

best to give you a decent first few days and first Christmas, Hope.'

This time, the baby gurgled.

And Amy really had to swallow the lump in her throat.

For a second the baby's dark blue eyes seemed to hold all the wisdom in the world.

How different her life could've been. But there was nothing she could do to change it now; all she could do was make the best of her situation. And, with Josh Farnham's help, do her best to make this poor baby's first few days as happy as possible.

When the baby dropped off to sleep again, Amy gently laid her on the makeshift towel bed, covered her up, and tried to work out what she needed to do next.

The intercom buzzed, and Amy rushed to get it before the noise woke the baby. 'Hello, it's Jane Richards again,' a tinny voice informed her.

'Come in,' Amy said, and buzzed her in before putting on the kettle. 'Can I make you tea or coffee?' she asked when the social worker came in laden with a Moses basket and an armful of carrier bags.

'Sorry, I can't stop for more than two minutes,' Jane said. 'I just wanted to drop these off for you, as I promised.' She put down the bags one by one, naming the contents. 'Moses basket, bedding, bottles, sterilising stuff, milk, nappies and newborn-size clothes.'

'Thanks.' The pile looked daunting, Amy thought. How could someone so tiny need so much stuff?

'The thanks are all mine,' Jane said. 'If you hadn't agreed to help out, I would've been really stuck. I did try to see if one of our foster carers could take Hope,

but everyone's so busy at this time of year. In reality
we're looking at the day after New Year.'

'Right.' Amy took a deep breath. Which meant she
was spending the next week with a baby that she'd have
to give back. It was a warning not to let herself bond
too deeply with Hope.

'So how's it going?' Jane asked.

'It's a lot harder than I thought it would be,' Amy
said. 'And I'm supposed to be a well-organised adult.
How on earth would a young, inexperienced mum cope
on her own?'

'She'd be struggling,' Jane said. 'I don't suppose the
police have found Hope's mum, yet?'

'Not that I've heard,' Amy said.

'Right. So what are you struggling with most?' Jane
asked. 'Is there anyone you can call on?'

'Only my neighbour,' Amy said. And she had the
strongest feeling that Josh might have some issues with
looking after a baby, too. Not that she could ask him
without either being rude and intrusive, which might
make him decide he didn't want to help, or telling him
about her past—and the last thing she wanted was for
him to start pitying her and seeing her in a different
light. 'As for what I'm struggling with, I'm worrying
that I'm doing *everything* wrong. I mean, I know I can
follow the instructions with the sterilising stuff and the
formula milk, and obviously I know to heat the milk in
a jug of hot water rather than in the microwave, but am
I feeding her enough and is she getting enough sleep?'
She grimaced. 'And she cries an awful lot more than I
was expecting. I'm not very good at getting her to feel
secure and happy.'

'Crash course,' Jane said. 'If the baby's crying, she

either wants feeding, a nappy change or a cuddle. Sing to her, rock her, hold her, dance with her—obviously I mean more like a slow dance than break-dancing.'

That made Amy smile. 'I don't think I can break-dance on my own, let alone with a baby in my arms.'

Jane grinned back. 'I guess. OK. Make the feeds in batches that'll be enough for a day's worth and keep them in the fridge, so all you have to do in the middle of the night is heat up the milk in a jug of hot water. Keep a note of the baby's feed times and how much she takes, and write down when she sleeps and how long. That'll help you see what her routine is. And obviously try to get some sleep when Hope sleeps, or you'll be exhausted by Boxing Day.' She scribbled down a phone number. 'If you're stuck, that's my mobile.'

'You're on duty over Christmas?'

'No,' Jane admitted, 'but without you I wouldn't know what to do with Hope, so I'm happy for you to call me if you need me.'

'Thanks,' Amy said.

'Good luck.'

And then she was on her own with the baby again. She just about had time to make up the Moses basket with the bedding, sterilise the bottles Jane had brought and make up the feeds before Hope woke, crying.

Amy could definitely tell the reason for this one: Hope needed a fresh nappy.

And then the baby was hungry.

And then she wanted a cuddle.

Time was rushing away. Amy knew that Josh would be back soon, and she hadn't even looked at the inside of her fridge, let alone started preparing something to eat.

'I'm supposed to be cooking dinner tonight,' Amy told the baby. Even if the shops hadn't closed early for Christmas Eve, she wouldn't have been able to go out and pick up a pizza in any case because she couldn't leave the baby alone. It was hardly fair to ask Josh to get a takeaway on the way back from his shift. 'We're going to have to go for something that can look after itself in the oven.'

The baby gurgled.

'You have no idea how weird this is,' Amy said. 'Josh and I smile and nod at each other if we pass in the hallway, and that's it. And now he's having dinner with me tonight and helping me look after you.'

No comment from Hope.

'But it's not a date,' Amy added. 'OK, so we're both single. But my past is messy and my future would be problematic for anyone who wants to date me. In fact, I'm just rubbish at picking men. Gavin was a liar and a cheat, and when it came to a crisis Michael walked away because I wasn't enough for him. So I'm better off forgetting all about romantic relationships.'

Though maybe looking after Hope might help her finally come to terms with the fact that she wasn't going to have a child of her own. To the point where she could reconnect with her friends—OK, she'd have a bit of grovelling to do, but she had a feeling that they'd understand when she explained why she'd gone distant on them. She could enjoy babysitting her friends' children and reading stories to them, and hopefully the joy would outweigh the ache in her heart.

'Besides, there's no reason why Josh should be interested in me,' she added. She'd felt that frisson of attraction when they'd accidentally touched while caring for the baby earlier, but she had no idea whether it was mutual. 'We might become friends. Which would be nice. But that's it,' she said firmly.

Hope gurgled then, as if to say, 'How do you know what he thinks?'

She didn't. But she did need his help, so she had no intention of doing or saying anything that might make him back away. 'It's just the way it is,' she said. 'And you, Missy, are going to have to go in the Moses basket for a few minutes, to let me put something together for dinner.'

In the end, Amy had to wait for Hope to fall asleep again. And then she worked at speed to peel and chop the veg, then put them in a casserole dish with a couple of chicken breasts and half a bottle of red wine.

By the time she'd finished, Hope was crying again. Amy suppressed a sigh and went through her mental checklist. Was the baby hungry, wet or just wanted a cuddle? And why was it so hard to work out which cry meant which?

Josh headed back to his flat after his shift. Right now all he wanted to do was to fall onto the sofa and watch something on TV that didn't require him to think too much. He was bone-deep tired, and wished he hadn't offered to help with the baby; but he had a feeling that Amy had only agreed to look after the baby because he'd promised to help. It would be pretty unfair of him to bail out on her now.

And she was cooking dinner for both of them. She hadn't said anything about dessert, but he didn't ex-actly have anything in his fridge that would pass muster. A bottle of wine was the best he could offer as his contribution.

He'd told her he'd be back for half-past eight—and it was twenty-five past now, so he didn't have time for a shower. He was pretty sure he wasn't sweaty and vile, and his hair had a mind of its own anyway, so it would be sticking out at odd angles within five minutes of him putting a comb through it. No point in wasting time.

Besides, this wasn't a date. It wasn't as if he had to dress up, or was trying to impress her by being smooth, suave and charming. Amy was his neighbour and he was simply helping with the baby who'd been abandoned on their doorstep.

At Christmas.

Not that you'd know it was Christmas, looking at his flat. It was even less Christmassy than Amy's was, because he hadn't even bothered putting any cards on the mantelpiece. He wondered if she loathed Christmas as much as he did. For him, Christmas Eve would always be the anniversary of the day his life imploded. When Kelly—who had been so adamant that she wanted to concentrate on her career rather than starting a family—had told him that she was pregnant. That the baby wasn't his. And that she was leaving him for the baby's father.

Josh had been too numb to believe it at first. But while he'd been saving lives and patching up wounds, Kelly had been packing her stuff, ready to leave him. Though in some ways she'd been fair. She'd been scrupulous only to pack things that were hers and to give him first dibs on anything they'd bought together; and she'd actually asked him to divorce her on the grounds of adultery rather than trying to make out that it was his fault or from joint 'irreconcilable differences'. She'd done as much as she could to make it easy on him.

Happy Christmas. Indeed. Every single radio station had been playing Christmas heartbreak songs, and when the third station in a row had been playing a song about a man pleading with his beloved to come home for Christmas, Josh had given up and switched off the radio—because he knew that Kelly wasn't coming home to him. Not for Christmas or at any other time.

He shook himself. It wasn't Amy's fault that his ex had changed her mind about wanting a baby and then decided that she didn't want to have said baby with him.

And it definitely wasn't Amy's fault that his family had reacted in typical Farnham fashion. Josh, the baby of the family, was a big fat failure. He was the only one who hadn't managed to combine a high-flying career with a perfect marriage and family. Obviously they hadn't actually *said* the words to his face, but Josh was aware of it with every look, every raised eyebrow, every whispered aside that was cut short the second he walked into the room.

This year, Kelly would be spending her first Christmas with her new family. Including the new baby.

And Josh genuinely wanted her to be happy. Now he'd got most of the hurt and anger out of his system, he could see that he hadn't been what Kelly had needed. If she'd stayed with him out of a sense of duty, she would've grown to hate him and it would all have grown miserable and messy. As it was, their divorce had been as amicable as possible. They'd sold the house and split the proceeds, and he'd bought the flat here six months ago.

But part of him was still in limbo.

And he really wanted to blot out Christmas Eve.

Except he couldn't. He'd made a promise, and he needed to keep it. He took a deep breath and went down the corridor to Amy's flat, then knocked on the door.

She opened it, looking slightly harassed, with Hope propped up against her shoulder. Clearly looking after the baby on her own had been hard going.

He suppressed the flush of guilt—he'd spent the last nine hours working his shift at the Emergency Department, not down at the pub taking part in several Christmas parties—and handed her the bottle of wine. 'I didn't know if you preferred red or white, so I played it safe.'

'Thank you. It's very nice of you, but you didn't need to.'

'You cooked dinner, so this is my contribution,' he pointed out. 'Something smells nice.'

'It's not very exciting, I'm afraid. Just a casserole and jacket potatoes, and all the veg are mixed in with the casserole.'

But it meant that he hadn't had to cook. 'It sounds lovely.'

'It was the lowest-maintenance thing I could think of,' she admitted wryly. 'Looking after Hope took an awful lot more time and energy than I expected.'

Yes, and if things had been different he would've been celebrating his first Christmas with his daughter—except his ex-wife's baby wasn't actually his daughter. He pushed the thought away. 'So I hear from my colleagues.' And this was his cue to play nice. Amy's brown eyes were so anxious, despite the calm she appeared to radiate. 'Here. My turn to cuddle Hope and keep her happy for a bit.'

And that was definitely gratitude in her eyes as she handed the baby over.

Though her hands brushed against his as they transferred the baby between them, and a frisson of desire flickered down his spine.

Inappropriate. Amy was his neighbour, and he was helping out with a tricky situation. That was it, he reminded himself. He wasn't going to hit on her and he wasn't going to let himself wonder how soft her hair was, or how her skin would feel against his.

'Can I get you a drink?' she asked.

'A glass of wine would be lovely right now,' he admitted. And it might distract him from all the ridiculous thoughts flickering through his head. Thoughts about how Amy's mouth was a perfect Cupid's bow, and wondering what it would feel like if he kissed her.

'Hard shift?'

He shrugged. 'It's always busy this time of year. Ignoring all the viruses and the elderly coming in with breathing problems, there are the falls—especially when it's icy like it has been tonight. And tonight the department will be full of people who drank too much at Christmas Eve parties and either ended up in a fight or fell and hurt themselves.' He gave her a wry smile. 'Tomorrow will be the people who had an accident carving the turkey, and a few more punch-ups because people who really shouldn't be in the same room together for more than ten minutes are forced to play nice for the whole day and it's too much for them, and the day after that will be the people who didn't store the leftover turkey properly and gave themselves food poisoning.'

'That,' she said, 'sounds a tiny bit cynical.'

'Experience,' he said, and grimaced. 'Sorry. I guess I'm a bit tired and not the best company.'

'It's fine.' She handed him a glass of wine. 'Come and sit down. Dinner will be five minutes.'

He went into the living room and blinked in surprise. 'You have a tree.'

She smiled. 'Yes—and you wouldn't believe how long it took me to put it up.'

'But you didn't have a tree this morning.'

'That's because I wasn't intending to be here for Christmas,' she said. 'I was meant to be spending this week in Edinburgh with some of my oldest friends, but they rang yesterday to call it off because they've gone down with the flu.' Amy shrugged. 'There didn't seem much point in putting up a tree when I wasn't going to be here. But now I am, and it's Hope's first Christmas.' Her fair skin flushed. 'It might sound a bit daft, but I wanted to put up a tree for her.'

'No, it's not daft. I get what you mean.' Josh paused. 'So the lack of a tree earlier wasn't because you don't like Christmas?'

'No.' She frowned. 'I take it you don't like Christmas, then?'

'It's not my favourite time of the year,' he admitted, and was relieved when she didn't push it and ask why. Though his mouth didn't seem to want to pay her the same courtesy, because he found himself asking questions. 'So you're not spending Christmas with your family?'

Amy shook her head. 'My brother lives in Canada, so my parents spend alternate Christmases here and over in Canada.'

'And this year is Canada's turn, right?'

'Right,' she agreed.

'So luckily for Hope that means you're here.'

'Yes.' Her expression was sombre when she looked at him. 'Things could have been very different.'

'But you found her in time.' He paused. 'Is there anything I can do to help?'

'I'm about to serve dinner, so if you want to settle Hope in her Moses basket, that'd be good.'

While Amy went to the kitchen, Josh put the baby in the Moses basket. Hope grizzled for a moment and then yawned and fell asleep.

Having dinner with Amy felt weirdly intimate. Like a date—though Josh couldn't even remember the last time he'd dated. He'd had a couple of offers that he'd turned down, and some well-meaning friends had tried to match-make, but he'd taken them to one side and explained that he appreciated their effort but he wasn't ready to date again.

Was he ready now?

And why on earth was he thinking about that?

'The food's very nice,' he said, to cover his awkwardness.

'Thank you.'

He didn't have a clue what to talk about, and it made him feel slightly flustered. He was used to making polite conversation to distract his patients or get more information out of them, or being out with colleagues that he'd known for so long that he didn't have to make small talk. This was definitely outside his comfort zone. Especially as he was becoming more and more aware of how attractive Amy was: not just those huge brown eyes, but the curve of her mouth, her pretty heart-shaped face and the slight curl to her bobbed hair. It made him itch to draw her, and he hadn't felt that urge for a long time either.

'So how long have you lived here?' he asked, trying to get his thoughts back to something much more anodyne and much, much safer.

'Eighteen months. You moved here last summer, didn't you?' she replied.

'Yes. It's convenient for the hospital, just a fifteen-minute walk.'

'It's about that to school, too,' she said. 'Just in the other direction.'

He remembered that she taught maths. 'Did you always want to teach?'

'I didn't want to be an accountant, an engineer or an actuary, so teaching was my best bet for working with maths—and actually it's really rewarding when the kids have been struggling with something and it suddenly clicks for them.' She smiled. 'Did you always want to be a doctor?'

'It was pretty much expected of me—Dad's a surgeon, Mum's a lawyer, my brother Stuart's an astrophysicist and my sisters are both lecturers.' He shrugged. 'One teaches history at Oxford and the other's in London at the LSE.'

'A family of high achievers, then.'

Yes. And he hadn't quite lived up to their expectations. He'd suggested becoming a graphic designer and going to art college instead of studying for his A levels, and the resulting row had left him very aware that he'd been expected to follow in his parents' and siblings' footsteps. In the end he'd settled on medicine; at least there'd been a little bit of drawing involved. And he liked his job. He liked being able to make a difference to people's lives. And he could still sketch if he wanted to.

When he had the time.

Which wasn't often.

Pushing the thought away, he asked, 'Have you heard anything from the police?'

'Not yet. Though Jane the social worker came round with supplies this afternoon.'

'So I notice. That Moses basket looks a little more comfy than a bunch of newspaper and a cardboard box.' His smile faded. 'That poor girl. I hope she's all right.'

'Me, too. And looking after a baby is a lot harder than I expected,' Amy admitted. 'Now I know what they mean about being careful what you wish for.'

He stared at her in surprise. 'You wanted a baby?'

She looked shocked, as if she hadn't meant to admit that, then glanced away. 'It didn't work out.'

That explained some of her wariness this morning. And it was pretty obvious to him that the baby situation not working out was connected with her being single. 'I'm sorry,' he said. 'I didn't mean to bring up bad memories.'

'I know. It's OK.' She shrugged. 'There's nothing anyone can do to change it, so you make the best of the situation, don't you?'

'I guess.' It was what he'd been doing since Kelly had left him. They'd sold their house and he'd bought this flat; it was nearer to work and had no memories to haunt him with their might-have-beens. 'In the circumstances, looking after Hope must be pretty tough for you.'

'It's probably been good for me,' she said. 'And it's kind of helping me to move on.' She bit her lip. 'I've been a bit of a cow and neglected my friends who were pregnant at the time or had small children.'

He liked the fact that she wasn't blaming anyone else for her actions. 'That's understandable if you'd only just found out that option was closed to you. You're human.'

'I guess.'

More than human. What he'd seen so far of Amy Howes told him that she was genuinely nice. 'And you're not a cow. If you were, you would've just told the police and the social worker to sort out the baby between them and pushed everyone out of your flat,' he pointed out. 'So did you ring any of your friends with small children to get some advice?'

'No. I don't want them to think I'm just using them. But I'm going to call them all in the first week of the New Year,' she said, 'and apologise to them properly. Then maybe I can be the honorary auntie they all wanted me to be in the first place and I was too—well, hurting too much to do it back then.'

'That's good,' Josh said. He wondered if helping to look after Hope would help him move on, too. Right now, it didn't feel like it; and if Amy had moved here eighteen months ago, that suggested she'd had a year longer to get used to her new circumstances than he had. Maybe his head would be sorted out by this time next year, then.

He almost told Amy about Kelly and the baby; but,

then again, he didn't want her to pity him, so he knew it would be safer to change the subject. 'What did the social worker have to say?'

'She gave me a very quick crash course in looking after a baby. She said if they cry it means they're hungry, they need a fresh nappy or they just want a cuddle, though I can't actually tell the difference between any of the different cries, yet,' Amy said dryly. 'Jane also told me to write down whenever Hope has milk and how much she takes, and her nap times, so I can work out what her routine is.'

'Sounds good. How's Hope doing so far?'

'She likes a lot of cuddles and she definitely likes you talking to her. Hang on.' She went over to the sideboard and took a notebook from the top, then handed it to him. 'Here. You can see for yourself.'

He looked through the neat columns of handwriting. 'I have to admit, it doesn't mean that much to me,' he said.

'Tsk, and you an uncle of three,' she teased.

'One's in Scotland and two are in Oxford,' he explained. 'I don't see them as much as I should.' It was another failing to chalk up to his list; and he felt guilty about it.

'Hey, you're a doctor. You don't get a lot of spare time,' she reminded him.

'I know, but I ought to make more of an effort.'

'It's not always easy. I don't see much of my brother.'

'He's in Canada, thousands of miles away,' Josh pointed out. 'And I bet you video-call him.'

She nodded.

'Well, then.' Amy was clearly a good sister. Just as Josh wasn't a particularly good brother. When was the last time he'd talked to Stuart, Miranda or Rosemary? He'd used his shifts as an excuse to avoid them.

'I guess,' she said, looking awkward. 'Can I offer you some pudding? It's nothing exciting, just ice cream.'

'Ice cream is the best pudding in the universe,' he said. 'Provided it's chocolate.'

'Oh, *please*,' she said, looking pained. 'Coffee. Every single time.'

He wasn't a fan of coffee ice cream. But he wasn't going to argue with someone who'd been kind enough to make him dinner. 'Coffee's fine,' he fibbed. 'And I'll wash up.'

'That's not fair.'

'You cooked.'

'But you were at work all day.'

He coughed. 'And you've spent hours on your own looking after a baby—that's hard work, even if you're used to it.' Then he flinched, realising what he'd said and how it sounded. 'Sorry. I didn't mean it to come out like that.'

'It's OK,' she said softly. 'I know you didn't mean it like that.'

But the sadness was back in her eyes. Part of him really wanted to give her a hug.

Though that might not be such a good idea. Not when he still felt that pull towards her. He needed to start thinking of her as an extra sister or something. A sister-in-law. Someone off limits. 'Let's share the washing up,' he said instead.

Though being in a small space with her felt even more intimate than eating at her bistro table.

'So what do you usually do on Christmas Eve?' he asked, trying to make small talk.

'Last year, I had my parents staying—and I guess I was busy convincing them that I was absolutely fine and settled here.'

'Were you really absolutely fine?' he asked quietly. Back then she'd been here for six months—exactly the same position that he was in now.

'Not really,' she admitted, 'but I am now.' She paused. 'I heard a couple of months back that my ex got married and he's expecting a baby.'

'The hardest bit is trying to be happy for them when you're feeling miserable yourself.'

Her eyes widened. 'That sounds like experience talking.'

He nodded. And funny how easy it was to talk to her, now he'd started. 'I split up with my wife last Christmas Eve.'

She winced. 'There's never a good time to break up with someone, but Christmas has to be one of the roughest. And the first anniversary's always a difficult one.' She squeezed his hand briefly, but it didn't feel like pity—more like sympathy and as if she'd been there herself, which he knew she had. 'If it helps to know, it does get easier. I know everyone says that time heals. I'm not sure it does that exactly, but it does help you deal with things a bit better.'

'I'm not still in love with Kelly,' he said. 'I want her to be happy. And I'm OK now about the fact it isn't going to be with me.'

'That's good. It's the same way I feel about Michael.'

It felt as if there was some subtext going on, but

Josh didn't trust his emotional intelligence enough to try to work it out.

She shook coffee grounds into a cafetière. 'Milk? Sugar?'

'Black, no sugar, please,' he said.

'Because you're a medic and you're used to grabbing coffee as quickly as you can?' she asked.

'No. It's a hangover from my student days,' he said with a smile. 'I shared a flat with some guys who weren't that good with checking that the milk was in date. The third time you make your coffee with milk that's off, you learn it's safer to drink your coffee black.'

She smiled back. 'I knew a few people like that in my student days, too.'

It was so easy to be with Amy, Josh thought. And it felt natural to curl up on the other end of her sofa, nursing a mug of coffee and listening to music while the baby was napping in the Moses basket.

'So what do you usually do at Christmas?' she asked.

'Work,' he said. 'It feels fairer to let my colleagues who have kids spend Christmas morning with their family.'

'That's nice of you.'

'Ah, but I get to party at New Year while they have to patch up the drunks,' he said with a smile, 'so it works both ways.'

Hope woke then, and started crying softly.

'I'll go and heat the milk,' Amy said.

Josh scooped the baby onto his lap and cuddled her until Amy came back with the milk. 'My turn to feed her,' he said.

When the baby had finished, he wrote the time and millilitres on Amy's chart.

'So at the moment she's feeding every two to three hours,' he said.

'Which means I'm not going to get a lot of sleep tonight.' Amy gave a wry smile. 'It's just as well I'm not going anywhere tomorrow, or I'd be a zombie.'

The sensible bit of his brain told him to back off and keep his mouth shut. The human side said, 'We could take shifts with her.'

'But you've been at work today—and I assume from what you said that you're working tomorrow.'

'And you've been on your own with her today, which pretty much counts as a full-time job,' Josh pointed out. 'If we take turns feeding her, we'll both get a four- or five-hour chunk of sleep.'

'So, what, you take her next door after the next feed and bring her back?'

'Or, if you don't mind me sleeping on your sofa, then we don't have to move her and risk unsettling her.'

Amy frowned. 'You can't possibly sleep on my sofa. It's way too short for you.'

'Student doctors learn to sleep on anything and be fully awake within seconds. I'll be fine,' he said. 'Let me go next door and grab my duvet.'

For a moment, he thought she was going to argue with him. But then she smiled, and he could see the relief in her eyes. 'Thanks. Actually, it'll be good not having the first night with her completely on my own. I'm paranoid I'm doing everything wrong.'

'Hey—she's new at this, too. If you're doing it wrong, she doesn't know any better. And she looks pretty content to me, so I'd say you're doing just fine.'

'Even when she cried non-stop for thirty minutes this afternoon—cried herself to sleep?'

He winced. 'That's tough on you. But don't blame yourself. She would probably have done exactly the same with me.' He smiled at her. 'I'll be back in a tick.'

CHAPTER THREE

WHAT HAVE I DONE? Amy asked herself as Josh went to collect his duvet.

Two years ago, she'd been in what she'd thought was a secure relationship, trying to start a family. A year ago she'd had a broken relationship, broken dreams and a broken heart. This year, she was on an even keel; but it seemed that she was going to be spending the next week with a man she barely knew and a baby who'd been left on their doorstep. It was an odd version of what she'd wished for.

Josh came back carrying a duvet. She wasn't sure if she felt more relieved or awkward that he was still fully dressed; clearly he intended to sleep in his ordinary clothes on her sofa. Though she guessed that went with the territory of his job.

He folded the duvet neatly over the back of her sofa. 'Anything you need me to do?'

'No. Hope's milk is on the top shelf of the fridge. But help yourself to anything you want.'

He smiled. 'Fifteen years ago, that would've guaranteed you an empty fridge.'

'That's what my colleagues at school say.' She smiled back. 'The boys leave crumbs everywhere, and the girls make chocolate mug cakes at three in the morning and leave everything in the sink.'

'Mug cakes?' He looked blank.

'You mix everything together in a mug and then stick it in the microwave. Three minutes later, you have cake,' she explained. 'I haven't actually tried it. But apparently it works perfectly when you really, really want cake at three in the morning.'

'Three minutes. Hmm. You can make a cheese toastie in that,' he said.

She smiled. 'If you get the munchies when it's your turn to feed Hope, feel free to make yourself a cheese toastie.'

He grinned back. 'If I do, I promise I'll clean up the crumbs.'

Almost on cue, Hope woke, wanting milk.

'I'll do the next feed,' Josh said when she'd finished. 'Go and get some sleep, Amy.'

Once Amy had showered and changed into her pyjamas, she lay awake in the dark, thinking that this was the Christmas she'd never expected. It must be just as weird for Josh, too, spending Christmas with an almost complete stranger—and tough for him, because his wife had left him on Christmas Eve last year and the memories had to hurt. But maybe looking after the baby would help distract him from some of the pain.

Part of her wanted to sleep for eternity, she was so tired—which was ridiculous, because she hadn't exactly done much all day. But looking after a newborn baby had been fraught with worry that had unexpectedly worn her out. Was she doing the right thing? How would she know if she was getting it wrong? What if the baby was ill and she hadn't spotted the signs? Or if she made such a mess of changing Hope that the baby ended up with nappy rash—and where would you be able to buy nappy rash cream on Christmas Day, when all the shops were shut?

The worries flickered through her head, stopping her from falling asleep. Part of her wanted to go and check that the baby was OK—but what if she woke Josh? He'd already worked a busy shift today at the hospital. Plus he was used to dealing with babies, and he'd said this was his shift; if he woke and found her checking on the baby, he might think she didn't trust him. And if that upset him enough to make him walk out on her without really discussing anything, the way Michael had walked out on her, how was she going to cope with the baby all on her own for a week?

Be careful what you wish for...

She'd longed for a baby. Now, she had exactly that. A baby to look after. For a week.

And it was terrifying.

Maybe Michael was right about her. She'd been too stupid to guess that Gavin might have given her a symptomless STD, so when she'd finally discovered the truth the treatment had been too late to prevent the damage to her Fallopian tubes. So it was her fault that she was infertile. Maybe she was too clueless to look after a baby, too. Why, why, why had she agreed to help?

She heard the baby start crying, and glanced at the clock. She hadn't even managed to sleep for five minutes. It was Josh's turn to feed the baby, but clearly he was in a deep sleep because the baby's cries grew louder.

Get up and see to the baby, she told herself sharply.

The poor little mite has nobody. Stop being so whiny and self-pitying and *get up*. You can't worry about not coping because you just *have* to. There isn't another option.

She dragged herself out of bed and stumbled into the living room. 'Shh, baby,' she whispered—but the baby just kept screaming.

Just as Amy scooped the baby out of the Moses basket, she heard Josh mumble, 'My turn. I've got this.'

'I'm awake now. I'll do it,' she said.

'We'll do it together,' Josh said. 'Cuddle the baby or do the milk?'

Amy inhaled the sweet, powdery scent of the baby.

A baby she couldn't afford to bond with. So it would be better not to get too close now.

'Milk,' she said, and handed Hope to him.

'Shh, baby,' he crooned.

On autopilot, Amy boiled the kettle and put the baby's bottle in a glass jug to heat the milk. She nearly scalded herself when she poured boiling water into the jug, and it splashed.

'Everything OK?' Josh asked, seeing her jump.

'Yes,' she fibbed. The last thing she wanted was for him to guess how stupid and useless she felt.

'Sorry I didn't wake sooner. I guess my shift took more out of me than I thought,' he said. 'I'm supposed to be helping. I've let you down.'

And then the penny dropped.

She wasn't the only one finding it hard to do this.

'You're fine,' she said. 'We're both new at this. I always tell my class, you learn more if you get it wrong first time.'

'I guess.' He sounded rueful. 'Except a baby is a

hell of a lot tougher than a page of maths problems. And, given how many babies I treat in the course of a month, I should be better at this.'

'There's a big difference between treating a baby and looking after one full time,' she reminded him. 'And didn't you say to me earlier that Hope doesn't know if we're doing it wrong?'

'Yeah. I'm glad I'm not doing this on my own,' he said.

He'd admitted it first, so it made it easier for her to say, 'Me, too. I never expected it to be this hard—you're desperate for sleep, but you're also too scared to sleep because you want to keep an eye on the baby.'

'All the *what ifs*,' he agreed. 'Being a medic is a bad thing, because you know all the worst-case scenarios and your mind goes into overdrive. You start thinking you're seeing symptoms when there aren't any. And then you're not sure if you're being ridiculously para- noid or if you really *are* seeing something.'

'And if you're not a medic, you look up stuff on the Internet and scare yourself stupid,' she said. 'Being a parent—even a stand-in—is way harder than I thought.'

'Especially the first night, when you don't have a clue what to expect,' Josh agreed.

'We're a right pair,' she said ruefully.

'No. We're a team,' Josh said.

And that spooked her even more. It was so long since she'd seen herself in a partnership that she didn't know how to react. Then she shook herself. He meant they were a team, not a couple. She was reading too much into this. To cover how flustered she felt, she shook a couple of drops of milk onto the inside of her wrist to check the temperature. 'I think it's OK for her, now.'

'Thanks. Go back to bed,' he said. 'I've got this.'

'Sure?' she checked.

'Sure.'

'OK.' And this time she felt more relaxed when she snuggled under the duvet—enough to let her drift into sleep.

The next time the baby cried, Amy got up and scooped up the Moses basket. 'Shh, baby,' she whispered. 'Two minutes.'

'OK?' Josh asked from the sofa, sounding wide awake this time.

He hadn't been joking about usually being fully awake in seconds, then.

'It's fine. It's my turn to feed her,' she said quietly. And the way they'd muddled through together earlier had given her confidence. 'Go back to sleep.'

She took the baby into the kitchen and cuddled her as she warmed the milk, then took the baby into her bedroom, kept the light down low, and cuddled the baby as she fed her.

This felt so natural, so right. But she had to remind herself sharply that this was only temporary and she couldn't let herself bond too closely to Hope—or start thinking about Josh as anything more than just a neighbour. By New Year, life would be back to normal again. They'd be back to smiling and nodding in the corridor, maybe exchanging an extra word or two. But that would be it.

Once the baby fell asleep again, Amy laid her gently back in the Moses basket and padded into the living room. Josh was asleep on the sofa, and this time he didn't wake.

* * *

A couple of hours later, when Hope started to grizzle again, Josh was awake in seconds.

'Shh, baby,' he whispered, and jiggled her one-handed against his shoulder as he set about making up a bottle.

When it had been his turn to deal with the baby, he'd made a complete hash of it. Not being used to listening out for a newborn, he'd slept through Hope's cries. But it turned out that Amy had been having the same kind of self-doubts that he had. Given that she'd seemed so cool, calm and collected, he'd been shocked. And then relieved. Because it meant that they were in this *together*.

And they made a good team.

To the point where he actually believed that he could do this—be a stand-in parent to an abandoned baby.

Then he realised he'd been a bit overconfident when he burped Hope and she brought up all the milk she'd just drunk. All over both of them.

He really hoped Amy didn't wake and find them both in this state. 'I dare not give you a bath,' he whispered to the baby. He knew she'd scream the place down, even if he managed to put water in the bath without waking Amy. But when he stripped off her sleep suit and vest, he discovered that luckily the baby wasn't soaked to the skin. Unlike him—but he was the adult and he'd live with it. He changed the baby into clean clothes, gave her more milk, then finally settled her back into the Moses basket.

Which left him cold and wet and smelling disgusting. He could hardly have a shower right now without waking Amy, and he couldn't go back to his own flat because he didn't have a key to Amy's. Grimacing, he stripped off his T-shirt and scrubbed the worst of the milk off his skin with a baby wipe.

Was this what life would've been like if he and Kelly had had a family? Would he have made as much of a mess of being a real dad as he was making of being a stand-in dad? Or maybe Amy was right and he was being too hard on himself. But he was seriously glad he wasn't looking after the baby on his own. It helped to be able to talk to someone else and admit that you didn't know what you were doing, and for them to say the same to you. And he was pretty sure now that he'd be able to get through this week—because Amy was on his team.

The next time Amy heard Hope crying, her eyes felt gritty from lack of sleep. Either the baby had slept a bit longer between feeds this time, or Amy had been too deeply asleep to hear her crying at the last feed.

When she stumbled into the kitchen to put the kettle on and checked the top shelf of the fridge, she realised it was the latter; Josh had done the last feed. He'd left her a note propped against the kettle. His handwriting was hard to read and she smiled to herself. Josh was definitely living up to the cliché of all medics having a terrible scrawl. Eventually she deciphered the note.

On early shift this morning—back for about 5.30 this evening—Merry Christmas, J

Christmas.
Amy hadn't planned to cook the traditional turkey

dinner; she hadn't seen the point of bothering when she was going to be on her own. But now she had unexpected company for dinner. She didn't have a turkey, but she did have the ingredients to make something nice. She could wrap a couple of chicken breasts in bacon, stir fry some tenderstem broccoli with julienned strips of butternut squash and carrot in butter and chilli, and make some baked polenta chips sprinkled with Parmesan.

'I forgot how much I enjoyed cooking,' she told the baby as she fed her. 'I haven't even had people over for dinner since I moved here. I always eat out with my friends. So maybe it's time to move on a bit more and start doing the things I enjoy again.'

The baby simply drank her milk and stared at Amy with those huge dark blue eyes.

'I've spent the last eighteen months living on autopilot,' Amy said. 'Don't you ever make that mistake, Hope. Life's for—well, enjoying.'

Though she was pretty sure that Hope's mum was having a thoroughly miserable Christmas. 'I hope we can find your mum,' she said softly. 'And I really hope we can do something to help her. I really don't know why she left you in our lobby—whether she knew me or Josh from somewhere, or whether it was a completely random choice—but I'm glad she did, because I think you're going to help us as much as we can help you.' And she was glad that Josh had moved in on her floor, because the reason she'd got through that first night with a baby was because of him.

Once she'd showered, washed her hair and dressed, she sent Josh a text.

Hope you're having a good shift. Alternative Christmas dinner this evening. Amy

And whether Hope was responding to her sunny mood and burst of confidence, Amy had no idea, but the baby seemed content, too; she wasn't quite as fractious and unsettled as she'd been the day before. To her relief, there wasn't one of the protracted crying sessions that had left Amy feeling hopeless and frustrated and miserable.

'Merry Christmas, baby,' she said softly. 'It isn't quite the one I think your mum would've liked for you, but hopefully the police are going to find her and reunite you in the next few days.'

Amy ate yoghurt and granola for breakfast, then looked at the small stack of presents beneath the tree. It felt odd, opening her Christmas presents all on her own. But she pushed away the melancholy before it could take hold. She intended to make the best of this Christmas, and she wasn't the only one on her own. It must be much harder for Josh in the circumstances.

Most of the envelopes contained gift vouchers, but one friend had given her the latest crime novel by one of her favourite authors, another had given her some nice Christmassy scented candles and another had bought her posh chocolates.

'That's my table decorations and dessert sorted for this evening,' she told the baby. 'And in the meantime you and I are going to curl up together on the sofa and watch a pile of Christmas movies.'

CHAPTER FOUR

AFTER HIS SHIFT, Josh showered and changed before going down the corridor to Amy's flat.

He felt a bit mean; she was cooking Christmas dinner for him, but he hadn't bought her even a token present. Then again, neither of them had expected this Christmas: for a newborn to be left on their doorstep, and then to be looking after a stranger's baby together when they barely knew each other. A present probably wasn't appropriate in the circumstances. Besides, even if the shops had been open, he didn't have a clue what kind of thing Amy liked—apart from coffee ice cream, and you could hardly wrap that and leave it under a tree. The wine he was carrying came from the rack in his kitchen, and the chocolates were a kind of re-gift. Which definitely made him feel like Scrooge.

'Merry Christmas,' he said when she opened the door in answer to his knock.

'Merry Christmas,' she said. 'I thought we'd eat at about half-past six, if that's OK with you?'

'More than OK. You have no idea how much I appreciate not having to cook for myself, or be forced to munch the leftover sausage rolls people brought in to the department because I'm starving but too tired even to make a cheese toastie,' he said with a smile. He handed her the chocolates and wine. 'This is my contribution for tonight.'

'You really didn't have to, but thank you.'

'And I have to admit that the chocolates are from the Secret Santa at work, which makes me a bit of a Scrooge for kind of re-gifting them,' he confessed.

'No, it just means that you don't usually have chocolate in the house and there aren't any shops open. And they're definitely appreciated,' she said, smiling back. 'How was your shift?'

'Let's just say we've renamed one of the twelve days of Christmas. "Five Turkey Carvers",' he said ruefully. 'I've done quite a bit of stitching up today.'

'Ouch,' she said.

'So how's our little one doing?' Then he realised what he'd said and felt his eyes go wide. 'Um,' he said. 'Sorry. I didn't quite…'

'I know,' she said quietly. 'It kind of feels like being part of a new family.'

'Even though she isn't ours, and we're not…'

'…a couple. Yeah,' she said.

Josh looked at her. Amy wasn't wearing a scrap of make-up, but she was naturally beautiful. He itched to sketch her, and it had been a long while since anyone had made him feel that way.

This was dangerous.

Part of him wanted to run; but part of him was intrigued and wanted more. To cover his confusion, he asked, 'Is there anything I can do to help?'

She shook her head. 'Hope's still asleep and I haven't started cooking dinner yet, so do you want a glass of wine or a cup of tea?'

'As it's Christmas, let's go for the glass of wine,' he said.

'And, as you said you wanted to help, you can open it.'

He followed her into the kitchen. When she handed him the corkscrew, his fingers brushed against her skin and it felt weird, as if he'd been galvanised. He was shockingly aware of her, but he didn't dare look at her because he didn't want her to guess what he was thinking. Had she felt it, too? And, if so, what were they going to do about it?

He shook himself mentally. They weren't going to do anything about it. They were neighbours. Acquaintances. And that was the way it was going to stay.

He opened the wine while she took two glasses from a cupboard; then he poured the wine before lifting his own glass and clinking it against hers. 'Merry Christmas.'

'Merry Christmas,' she echoed.

'I haven't bought you a present,' he said, 'and I feel kind of bad about it.'

'I haven't bought you one, either,' she said. 'I did think about wrapping up a bottle of wine for you or something, but it didn't feel appropriate.'

'Considering we hardly know each other and don't have a clue what each other likes,' he agreed.

'We haven't bought Hope anything, either,' she said, 'but it's fine. Christmas isn't really about the presents, and perhaps what we're actually giving each other is a better Christmas than we were expecting.'

'You know,' he said, 'I think you might be right. You're a wise woman, Amy Howes.'

'It goes with the territory of being a maths teacher,' she said with a smile.

He liked her sense of humour. And, actually, the more he talked to her, the more he liked a lot of other things about her. Which again set his alarm bells ringing. He wasn't supposed to be thinking like that. He was newly divorced. Not in a place to start anything with anyone.

'Maybe,' he said, 'we can make a kind of present for Hope. A book of her days with us. Photographs, that kind of thing.'

'Add in her feed and sleep charts, too?' Amy said. 'That's a really nice idea. And then she's got something to keep.'

'So how has it been with the baby today?' he asked.

'Easier than yesterday. We've been watching Christmas movies,' she said.

'Sounds like a good plan.'

'*Love Actually* is one of my favourite films. And you really can't top the Christmas lobster.'

Then Amy remembered that one of the storylines in the movie involved an affair. Talk about rubbing salt in his wounds. How could she have forgotten that Josh's wife left him for another man, last Christmas Eve? 'Sorry. I just put my foot in it. I didn't mean to make you feel bad.'

'I'm not a fan of romcoms,' Josh said, 'and you haven't put your foot in it—even though I get what you're saying. This is way better than Christmas was last year, believe me.'

Which didn't make her feel any less guilty. Just about anything would be an improvement on his last

Christmas. 'Maybe I should start prepping dinner,' she said awkwardly.

'As the baby's asleep, is there anything I can do?'

'You can keep topping up the wine and chat to me in the kitchen, if you like,' she suggested.

'I'd like that. Funny, two days ago we were almost complete strangers,' he said, 'and now we're spending Christmas together.'

'As a kind of blended family with a baby who's a complete stranger, too,' she said.

'I still don't know anything about you,' he said, 'other than that you're a maths teacher and you have a brother who lives in Canada.'

'And you're an emergency department doctor who's the youngest of four.' She shrugged. 'OK. So what do you want to know? I'm thirty.'

'I'm thirty-two,' he said.

Amy started chopping the carrots into matchsticks.

'And you obviously enjoy cooking—or at least you're good at it,' Josh said.

She smiled. 'Thank you, and I do. Does that mean you don't?'

'I'd rather wash up than cook,' he said. 'Obviously I can cook a few basics—you wouldn't survive as a student unless you knew how to make stuff like spaghetti Bolognese and cheese toasties—but spending all that time making something that people will wolf down in two seconds flat and then forget about...' He smiled. 'Or maybe that's the medic in me talking.'

'So food's fuel rather than a pleasure?'

'At work, yes,' he admitted. 'Shamefully, I eat a chocolate bar on the run for my lunch way more often than I ought to.'

'So what sort of things do you like doing outside work?' Amy grimaced. 'I'm sorry. This sounds like a terrible speed-dating sort of grilling.'

'Speed-dating,' he said, 'is something I've never actually done.'

'Me neither,' she agreed. 'Though I guess, when you get to our age, it's probably about your only option for meeting someone, if you haven't already clicked with someone you met at work or with a friend of a friend at a party.'

'And if you're in a job with unsocial hours, work means that half the time you're not on the same shift and it's hard to find a time when you can actually do something together,' he added. 'Though I think being set up with a friend of a friend is worse than dating someone at work, because then if it doesn't work out it makes things a bit awkward with your friend. You feel a bit guilty and as if you've let your friend down.'

'That sounds like experience talking,' Amy said.

Josh wrinkled his nose. 'I did have a couple of well-meaning friends try to set me up, earlier this year, but I told them I just wasn't ready.'

She nodded. 'I know what you mean. It was a while before I could face dating after I split up with Michael; then, after that, I just didn't meet anyone I could click with.'

Though she had a feeling that she could click with Josh, given the chance. It surprised her how much she liked him and how easy he was to talk to.

'One of my friends tried speed-dating a few months back,' Josh said. 'He tried to talk me into going with him, but it sounded a bit too much like a meat market for me. He did say afterwards that all the women he'd met had had a massive list of questions they'd prepared earlier, and it felt like the worst kind of job interview.'

'I guess asking questions is a quick way of getting to know someone,' she said.

He smiled at her. 'Maybe we should look at one of those lists. It'll save us having to think up our own questions.'

'Good idea,' she said, carefully separating the tenderstem broccoli and adding it to her pile of stir-fry veg before starting on the butternut squash.

Josh took his phone from his pocket and flicked into the Internet. 'Here we go. What you do at work? Well, we already know that about each other. Where are you from?' He frowned. 'That's pretty irrelevant.' He flicked further down the list. 'OK. Let's try this one. What's the one thing about yourself that you'd like me to know?'

'I don't have a clue,' she said.

'Me, neither. Let's skip to the next one.' He grimaced. 'That's all about your last relationship. It's too intrusive. Same as whether you're looking to get married.' He shook his head. 'I can't believe you'd actually ask a complete stranger if they're looking to get married when you're thinking about maybe dating them for the first time. I mean—you might be completely incompatible. Why would you talk about marriage that early on?'

'Maybe that's the point of speed-dating. To speed everything up,' Amy said. 'If you want to settle down but the person you're thinking about dating doesn't, you're both kind of wasting each other's time.'

'That question still feels wrong.' He scrolled down

the page. 'This is a bit more like it. What do you do for fun?'

'Music,' she said promptly. 'Not clubbing—I like live music, whether it's a tiny venue where there's only enough room for a couple of dozen people listening to someone playing an acoustic guitar, or a big stadium with a massive stack of amps and a light show.'

'What kind of music?' he asked.

'All sorts—everything from pop to rock. I'm not so keen on rap,' she said, 'but I love the buzz you get from going to a concert and singing along with the rest of the audience. What about you?'

'I tend to listen to rock music when I'm running,' he said. 'Something with a strong beat that keeps me going.'

'So you're a runner?'

'Strictly outdoor. I like the fresh air, and the views,' he said, 'rather than being cooped up in a gym on a treadmill where you just see the same patch of wall for half an hour or so.'

'Park or river?' she asked.

'If it's wet, river,' he said, 'purely because you're less likely to slide on the mud and rick your ankle. If it's dry, definitely the park because it's lovely to see all that green, especially in spring when all the leaves are new and everything looks fresh. And if I worked regular hours I'd definitely have a dog to run with me.' He shrugged. 'I don't have a dog because my hours aren't regular and it wouldn't be fair to leave the dog alone for so long.'

'You look like a Labrador person,' she said.

He nodded. 'Or a spaniel. Or a Dalmatian—where I lived before, our neighbour had this amazing Dalmatian who used to smile at me. And it really was a friendly greeting rather than baring his teeth, because his tail was wagging so hard the whole time.'

Amy could see the wistfulness on his face. The breakup of his marriage had cost him more than just his relationship.

'How about you?' he asked.

'No to the running. I like spinning classes,' she said, 'because I don't have to worry about riding a bike in traffic and I don't have to drag myself outside when it's wet.'

'That's reasonable—though, actually, running in the rain is great. Dog or cat?'

'Dog,' she said. 'But, like you, I don't want to leave a dog cooped up alone in my flat all day. So I make the most of it when I go to see my parents—they've got Border terriers.'

He continued scrolling through the list of questions. 'Some of these definitely sound more like the sort of thing you'd ask in a job interview. Why would you ask someone if they have a five-year plan?'

'Because you want to know if they're ambitious and would put their career before your relationship; or find out if they're the kind of person who drifts along and gets stuck in a bit of a rut,' she suggested.

'Which in turn probably means your relationship will end up in a rut, too.' He rolled his eyes. 'There have to be easier ways of getting to know what a person's like.'

'In the space of three minutes, or however long it is you have on a speed date? I don't think you have a choice but to ask intrusive questions,' she said.

'I give up on the list. What sort of thing would you ask?'

'About their interests,' she said. 'Dating someone who wanted to spend their whole weekend playing sport or watching sport would be pretty wearing.'

'Yes, because when would you get time to do other things together?' he agreed.

'In the evenings, maybe—something like the cinema?' she suggested.

'I haven't been to the cinema in way too long,' he said. 'I tend to end up waiting for things to come out on DVD, and even then I haven't caught up with all the latest releases, and I've got a pile of stuff I've been meaning to see and haven't had time for.'

'So why don't you go to the cinema?' she asked. 'Because you like the kind of things that nobody else does, so you'd have to go on your own?'

'Art-house movies in a foreign language?' he asked. 'No, it's more that my duty roster tends to get in the way and everyone's already seen the film before I get a chance. I like the big sci-fi blockbusters.'

'Ah. Now I have a question for you. Team Cap or Team Iron Man?' she asked.

'Team Cap,' he said promptly, and she gave him a high five.

'So you like the same kind of films as I do?' he asked.

'Yup. I do like romcoms as well, but I've always been a sci-fi geek. And I bought myself the one that came out last week as an early Christmas present. I know it's not strictly a Christmas movie, but maybe we could watch it tonight.'

'And we can pause it if Hope needs a nappy change or a feed. Great idea.' He smiled at her. 'So we like the same kind of films and music. How about TV?'

'Cop dramas,' she said. 'That's my guilty pleasure. All the Scandinavian noir stuff.'

'Again, I have to watch them on catch-up half the time, but me too,' he said.

'Right. Crosswords or number puzzles?'

He groaned. 'Neither. I'm assuming that you'd go for the maths problems?'

'Absolutely.' She smiled. 'Reading—fiction or non-fiction?'

'Non-fiction,' he said promptly, 'and it's usually medical journals. You?'

'Crime fiction,' she said. 'I guess it's because I like trying to solve the puzzles.'

'Beach holiday or climbing a mountain?' he asked.

'Neither—city break or road trip for me,' she said. 'I like exploring new places and seeing the sights. You?'

'I like the sound of the road trip,' he said. 'I'd love to see New England in the fall. And the hot springs and waterfalls at Yosemite.'

'I'd guessed you'd be bored on a beach, but you strike me as a mountain-climbing type,' she said.

'Not so much mountains,' he said, 'but I did do the coast-to-coast walk for charity, one year, and I loved every second of it—even the blisters.'

'I'm afraid the best I've done in the charity stakes is to make cakes and sponsor friends who do the ten-K runs,' Amy said.

'The main thing is that the money's raised. It doesn't matter who does what,' he said.

Just as Amy finished prepping dinner, Hope woke.

'Well, hello, Munchkin,' he said, and scooped the baby out of her Moses basket. 'So it's Uncle Joshy's turn to feed you.'

'I'll bring the milk in,' Amy said.

When she took the warmed milk in, Josh was sitting on the sofa, talking to the baby in a low voice and letting her wrap her tiny fist round his little finger. The sight put a lump in her throat. Josh was so warm and kind. He'd make a fabulous father one day—but that made him off limits for her, so she'd have to ignore the attraction she felt towards him. If he wanted children, she couldn't take his future away from him like that. And, given the way he was acting with the baby right now, she was pretty sure he'd want a family of his own one day.

Josh took the bottle of milk from Amy. 'Thanks.'

'No problem.'

Hope closed her eyes in bliss as she drank the milk. And it was strange how natural this felt, having a warm little weight in the crook of his arm. In another life, this could've been his baby...

He glanced at Amy. For all his scorn about the speed-dating questions, they had at least established that they had quite a few interests in common. And the more he got to know her, the more he liked her. It had been a while since he'd met someone he felt he could really be himself with.

'Hey. Smile,' she said, and held up her camera.

'For Hope's book?'

'You bet.'

'Then I ought to be sitting with the Christmas tree behind me.' He stood up, without disturbing Hope or stopping her drinking her milk, and moved so Amy could take a more Christmassy photo of them together. 'I'll take one of you with her later, too.'

'Thanks.'

She laid the table while he fed the baby. 'Sorry, it's not going to be a proper Christmas dinner, and I don't have any crackers or party hats—but I do have a Christmas scented candle.'

'Sounds good. Anything I can do to help?'

'You already are,' she said. 'And you've been at work all day. Just chill with the baby.'

This really, really felt like being part of a new little family.

Josh knew he was going to have to keep a tight grip on his imagination, because that so wasn't happening. Yes, he found Amy attractive; but the last thing he wanted to do was to have a fling with her and then for it all to go wrong and make things awkward if he bumped into her in the lobby or the corridor. They needed to keep things strictly platonic, he reminded himself.

And that was what stopped him going to chat to her in the kitchen again when the baby had finished her feed and he'd burped her.

Though sitting there watching the baby fall asleep made his fingers itch to sketch her. When he wrote all the details of the feed down in Amy's notebook, he couldn't resist flicking to the very back of the book. It didn't matter that the paper was lined and he was using a pen rather than a pencil; he gave into the urge and sketched the sleeping baby. And maybe this was something he could add to Hope's book. Something personal.

He was so wrapped up in what he was doing that he didn't notice Amy standing beside him, carrying a glass of wine.

'That's seriously good,' she said. 'Did you ever think about being an artist instead of a doctor?'

His big dream. The one that had been squashed before it had had a chance to grow. For once he answered honestly. 'Not in a family of high achievers,' he said wryly. 'Art wasn't quite academic enough for them.'

'Your parents didn't support you?' She sounded shocked. Clearly her family was the sort to encourage her to follow her dreams rather than insist that she trod the path they'd mapped out for her.

'They didn't like the idea of me going to art school,' Josh admitted. 'They said the world had changed a lot in the last generation and there weren't that many jobs in art.' At least not ones that paid well. Though he ought to be fair about it. 'I guess they had a point.'

'What made you choose medicine instead?' she asked.

'Studying biology meant I could still draw,' he said. 'Besides, art is something I can do for me.'

'Do you do much?'

That was the killer question. He smiled wryly. 'It hasn't quite worked out that way.'

'Make the time, Josh,' she said softly. 'If drawing makes you happy, make the time for it.'

Kelly had never suggested that to him.

But then again, the real him hadn't been enough for her, any more than it had been enough for his family—or Kelly would've had her baby with him instead of with another man.

He pushed the thought away. Now wasn't the time to be maudlin or filled with regrets.

'Dinner's about ready,' she said.

'Perfect timing. Munchkin here's set to sleep for

a couple of hours,' he said. 'Can I bring anything in for you?'

'No, but you can light the candle, if you want. The matches are in the top drawer of the cupboard over there.'

He lit the candle and sat down while she brought in the dishes.

'This is fabulous,' he said after the first taste of the polenta chips sprinkled with parmesan.

'Thanks. It's been a while since I've made these,' she said.

'You told me to make the time for doing something I love—that goes for you, too,' he said gently.

'I guess. I'll make more of an effort in the new year, as long as you promise to do the same.'

'I will,' he agreed. 'I've been thinking—do you reckon the baby's mother picked our block of flats at random?'

'Maybe,' Amy said. 'Are you thinking she didn't?'

'She rang your doorbell. That might've been chance—but supposing you knew her?'

Amy shook her head. 'That's unlikely. I don't know anyone who's pregnant.'

'But we think she's young and scared, right?' he asked, warming to his theory. 'The chances are, she hid her pregnancy from just about everyone. But maybe she knew you from school.'

'I didn't recognise the handwriting, so I don't think she's anyone I teach,' Amy said. She frowned. 'But then again…'

'What if she wrote the note with her non-writing hand?' Josh suggested.

'Or what if,' Amy said slowly, 'she's someone I don't

teach, so I've never really seen her handwriting properly? Now I think about it, there's a girl in my form who's gone very quiet over the last few months. I did have a confidential word with her mum, but she said Freya was being difficult because her new partner had just moved in.'

'It happens,' Josh said. 'How old is she?'

'Fifteen.'

'Then maybe, if she's unhappy at home, she's blotting it out with the help of a boyfriend.'

'I don't think she has a boyfriend,' Amy said. 'At least, not one who's at school. You normally hear the kids talking and work out who's seeing who.'

'Does she look as if she's put on weight?'

Amy thought about it. 'She always wears baggy clothes so it's hard to tell. But, now you mention it, she does look as if she's put on weight. I assumed she was comfort-eating because she was unhappy at home and I didn't want to make her feel any worse by drawing attention to it. Teens are under such pressure when it comes to body image. I didn't want to say something that would make her start starving herself. But I have noticed her dashing off to the loo in the middle of form time over the last term, and I was going to have a quiet word with her next term to check she didn't have an eating disorder.'

'Or maybe,' Josh said, 'she was dashing off to the loo because she was in the last trimester and the baby's weight was putting pressure on her bladder.'

'That's a good point. But why didn't she say anything to me?'

'In the cases I've seen at work,' Josh said, 'where the mum's under age and scared, she's either been in denial about the situation or too scared to tell anyone in case she gets into trouble.'

'That's so sad,' Amy said. 'To be young and scared and not know where to go for help.'

'She didn't say anything to you,' Josh said. 'But it would make sense that she'd leave the baby with someone she knew would help and do the right thing for the baby.'

'Agreed. But this is all speculation,' she said. 'We don't have any proof.'

'And we have to do this through the proper channels,' Josh added. 'If our theory's right, then we could do more harm than good if we go rushing over to see her.'

'Plus we don't have a car seat or anyone to keep an eye on Hope while we go and see her,' she agreed. 'Jane, the social worker, will know the right way to go about this. We can talk to her about it.'

'Tomorrow's Sunday—Boxing Day—and then Monday and Tuesday are bank holidays, so she won't be in the office for a few days,' Josh pointed out.

'She did give me her mobile number, but it was for emergencies—and, because this is a theory and we don't have any real proof, it doesn't really count as an emergency.' Amy frowned. 'I guess it'll have to wait a few days.'

'Or maybe you could text Jane tomorrow?' he suggested. 'Then she'll have the information and she can decide if she wants to take it further any earlier.'

'Good idea,' she said.

'I'm off duty tomorrow.' He gave her a wry smile. 'It would've been nice to take the baby out to the park, but as she doesn't have a coat and we don't have a pram or even a sling, and there's not going to be anywhere open tomorrow where we can buy something for her, I guess we're stuck.'

'It feels a bit like being snowbound,' Amy said, 'but without actually being snowed in.'

'And you haven't left your flat for two days.' Guilt flooded through him. She'd had the majority of the burden of worrying about the baby. 'Sorry, I should've thought of that earlier and suggested you went out to get some fresh air or something.'

'No, it's fine, but probably tomorrow I could do with some fresh air,' she admitted, 'if you don't mind looking after Hope on your own for a few minutes.'

'Sure. That's no problem.'

After dinner, they curled up on the sofa and watched the sci-fi film together. A couple of times, Josh's hand accidentally brushed against Amy's and he seriously considered letting his fingers curl round hers.

But then again, she'd said she wasn't ready for another relationship, and he knew his own head was still in a bit of a mess.

He was definitely attracted to Amy. But how could he trust that love wouldn't go wrong for him again, the way it had with Kelly? It was better to stick to just being friends. That would be safer for all of them.

'I guess it's time to get some sleep,' Amy said when she'd fed Hope and noted everything down. 'I'll do the next feed.'

'Sure?'

'Sure. Feel free to leave the TV on as long as you want, though. You won't be disturbing me.'

'OK. I'll get my duvet,' he said.

'Take my key with you,' she said. 'Merry Christmas, Josh.'

'Merry Christmas, Amy.'

For a moment he thought she was going to rise on tiptoe and kiss him, and his whole body seemed to snap to attention. What would it feel like, her lips against his skin? Would her mouth be as soft and sweet as it looked? And what if he twisted his head to the side so her mouth connected with his instead of with his cheek?

He was shocked to realise how much he wanted it to happen.

And even more shocked to realise how disappointed he was when she simply smiled and headed for the bathroom instead.

Oh, help. He really had to get a grip. He and Amy were neighbours. Maybe they were on the way to being friends. This whole thing of looking after the baby together was seriously messing with his head. He didn't want to risk his heart again. End of. So he was going to be sensible.

Completely sensible.

CHAPTER FIVE

Boxing Day—Sunday

'Josh. *Josh.*'

He was awake instantly, and he could hear the note of panic in Amy's voice. 'What's happened?'

'It's Hope. She feels really hot and she hardly drank any milk just now. I think there's something wrong.'

'Hold on. Where's the light? I'll take a look at her.'

She switched on one of the lamps in the living room.

Josh took the baby from Amy's arms and gently examined her. 'You're right—she does feel hot.'

'I have one of those ear thermometers. Maybe we should take her temperature and see how bad it is?' Amy suggested.

'Unfortunately, those thermometers are too big for a newborn baby's ears,' he said. 'We need a normal digital thermometer. I've got one in my bathroom— I'll go and get it.'

Amy frowned. 'But surely you can't stick a thermometer in a baby's mouth?'

'Nope—you stick it under her armpit,' he said.

'Oh.' Amy looked at him. 'Anything I can do?'

'Strip her down to her nappy and a vest while I get

the thermometer, then hold her for me and talk to her,' he said. 'And if you've got some cooled boiled water, we'll try and get her to drink some.'

When he checked the baby's temperature, he wasn't happy with the reading. 'It's thirty-eight degrees. It's a bit high, but a baby's temperature can go up and down really quickly because at this age their bodies haven't worked out yet how to control their temperature. I'm ninety-five per cent sure this is nothing serious, because the soft spot at the top of her head isn't sunken and she isn't floppy,' he reassured Amy. Though that left a five per cent chance that this was the early stages of something nasty. 'But, given that we don't really know the circumstances of her birth, there's a chance she might have a bacterial infection,' he said. And in that case she would get worse. Quickly, too, though he wasn't going to worry Amy about that now. 'The only way to find out is by a blood test and urine analysis, which I can't do here.'

'So we need to take her to hospital?' Amy asked.

He sighed. 'I'd rather not have to do that, with all the viruses going around, but babies this young can get very unwell quite quickly, so if it *is* an infection I'd want her treated for it as soon as possible. Though, at this time of the morning, the department will be relatively quiet, so we won't have to wait too long.'

'Just take our turn with the drunks who've fallen over after a party or had a punch-up?' she asked wryly.

He smiled. Clearly she'd remembered his grumpy assessment of the seasonal waiting room. 'Yes, but she'll be triaged. We prioritise when we see our patients, depending on their symptoms and how old they are. Hope will get seen really quickly because she's a newborn with a temperature.'

'We don't have a car seat or a pram. How are we going to get her to hospital?' Amy asked.

'We can't risk taking her in the back of the car in her Moses basket,' Josh said. 'Apart from the fact it's illegal and we have departmental guidelines, so we can't let anyone take a child from hospital without an appropriate seat, I also know most accidents take place within a mile of a home. We're going to have to call an ambulance.'

'OK. I'll get Hope dressed again while you call the ambulance, and then I'll throw on some clothes. Give me two minutes.'

She was as good as her word, he noticed, taking only a couple of minutes and not bothering with make-up or anything like that. Practical. He liked that.

'They'll be here in another five minutes,' he said. 'I told them we'd wait in the lobby.'

Between them, they tucked Hope into her Moses basket; Amy grabbed the notebook so they had a record of everything the baby had drunk, and they waited in the lobby until they saw the ambulance pull up outside.

'Josh! You're the last person I expected to see—nobody thought you were even dating anyone, let alone had a new baby,' the paramedic said.

Oh, help. He could really do without any gossip at work. 'The baby's not mine,' he said hastily.

The paramedic looked intrigued. 'So you're helping your...' she glanced at Amy '...friend.'

'The baby's not mine, either,' Amy said. 'We're looking after her temporarily.'

The paramedic's eyes rounded. 'Together?'

'We're neighbours,' Josh added. 'And you might have seen something about the baby in the news.'

'Oh, hang on—is this the Christmas Eve doorstep baby?'

'Yes. Her name's Hope,' Amy said, 'and she's got a temperature.'

'Thirty-eight degrees, axillary,' Josh said, 'and we stripped her off and gave her cooled boiled water, but we don't have any liquid paracetamol. I need blood tests and urine analysis to rule out a bacterial infection. She's not floppy or drowsy so I'm not panicking, but given her age and the fact that we don't know the circumstances of her birth or anything about her medical history...'

The paramedic patted his arm. 'Josh, you're off duty. Stop worrying. We'll handle it. Right now you count as a patient, not staff. Are you coming in with her?'

'We both are,' Josh said.

It was the first time Amy had ever travelled in an ambulance. And even though Josh was able to answer most of the paramedic's questions and she had the notes about Hope's feeds, it was still a worrying experience.

Especially when the paramedic put a tiny oxygen mask on the baby.

'What's wrong?' Amy asked.

'It's a precaution,' Josh said. Clearly he could tell how worried she was, because he took her hand and squeezed it to reassure her. Somehow her fingers ended up curled just as tightly round his.

The drive to hospital was short, but it felt as if it

took for ever. And when Hope was whisked into cubicles the second they arrived, with the doctor acknowledging them but asking them to wait outside, Amy's worries deepened.

'It's routine,' Josh said. 'They'll be taking blood and urine samples to check if she's got an infection.'

'But why can't we stay with her?' Amy asked. 'I mean, I know we're not her actual parents, but…'

'I know.' His fingers tightened round hers. 'As I said, it's routine and we're just going to get in the way. We need to let the team do their job.'

'You work here. Doesn't that make a difference?' Amy asked.

He shook his head.

And then a really nasty thought struck her. He'd said that new babies couldn't regulate their temperatures that well. If Hope had an infection and her temperature shot up… Could she die?

Time felt as if it had just stopped.

'Josh. Tell me she's not going to…' The word stuck in her throat.

He looked at her, and she could see her own fears reflected in his blue eyes.

'We have to wait for the test results,' he said.

The baby wasn't theirs—or at least was only theirs temporarily—but right then Amy felt like a real parent, anxious for news and trying not to think of the worst-case scenarios. Any tiredness she felt vanished under the onslaught of adrenaline. This was the only chance she might have to be a parent. And what if she lost something so precious—the baby she hadn't asked for but was beginning to fall in love with, despite her promises to herself not to let herself get involved?

'Amy,' Josh said softly. 'It's going to be all right. Alison—the doctor who is looking after her—is one of my most experienced juniors. She'll spot any problem and know how to treat it.'

'I guess.'

He must have heard the wobble in her voice, because this time he wrapped his free arm around her and held her close. 'It's going to be OK.'

She leaned back and looked at him. 'You look as worried as I feel.'

'A bit,' he admitted wryly. 'My head knows it's going to be fine. If there was anything really serious going on, Alison would've come out to see us by now.'

'But?'

'But my heart,' he continued quietly, 'is panicking. This must be what it's like to be a parent. Worrying if the baby is OK, or if you're missing something important.'

She nodded. 'I'm glad you're with me. Knowing I'm not the only one feeling like this makes it feel a bit less—well—scary.'

'Agreed.' Though she noticed he was still holding her; clearly he was taking as much comfort from her nearness as she was from his.

And then finally the curtain swished open.

'Hey, Josh. We've done bloods and urine, to rule out bacterial infections,' Alison said. 'And I gave her a proper cord clip. How on earth did you manage to change her nappy round that thing?'

'A mixture of necessity and practice,' Amy said wryly.

'Ouch,' Alison said. 'Well, you know the drill, Josh. We'll have to wait for the test results before we can tell if we need to admit her—and, given all the viruses in the hospital right now, hopefully we won't have to do that. But you can sit with the baby now while we wait for the results to come back, if you like.'

'Yes, please. And no doubt you have potential fractures in the waiting room that need looking at,' Josh said. 'Sure. We won't hold you up any longer.'

When Alison had closed the cubicle curtain behind her, Josh turned to Amy. 'We can't pick her up and hold her,' Josh said, 'because our body warmth will put her temperature up.' Which meant they had to resort to taking turns in letting Hope hold a finger in her left hand, because Hope's right hand was hooked up to a machine.

'So what does this machine do?' Amy asked.

'It's a pulse oximeter. It measures the oxygen levels in her blood,' Josh explained, 'so we know if there's a problem and we need to give her some extra oxygen through a mask, like they did in the ambulance. It's all done by light shining through her skin and it doesn't hurt her.' He was used to explaining the situation, but it felt odd to be on the other side of it, too.

'Right. Are those figures good news or bad?' she asked, gesturing to the screen.

He analysed them swiftly. 'Good. I'm happy with her oxygen sats and her pulse rate.'

Amy bit her lip. 'She's so tiny, Josh, and we're supposed to be looking after her. What if…?'

'If she has an infection, she's in the right place for us to treat it,' Josh reassured her. 'She'll be fine.'

Two hours later, the baby's temperature was down to a more normal level. The results of the blood tests had come back, and to their relief there was no sign of any bacterial infection.

'I'm pleased to say you can take her home. Just keep an eye on her and give her some liquid paracetamol every four to six hours—you know the safe dose for a baby that age,' Alison said to Josh. 'How are you getting home?'

'Ambulance, I guess,' Josh said. 'We don't have a car seat for her. The social worker obviously didn't guess we might have to rush her to hospital.'

'So you've got almost nothing for her?' Alison asked.

'Just the very basics—this Moses basket, some clothes and formula milk,' Amy confirmed.

'Poor little mite. She's lucky you found her,' Alison said. 'And that you could look after her.'

'We're neighbours,' Josh said quickly.

Alison looked at their joined hands and smiled.

Josh prised his fingers free. 'And friends. And worried sick about the baby.'

'She's going to be fine,' Alison said. 'I'll let the ambulance control know that you can go whenever they're ready.'

This time the journey wasn't as terrifying, and Hope slept through the whole thing. Though Amy felt as if she'd never, ever sleep again when she let them back into her flat. 'I'll sit up with her.'

'I'll keep you company,' he said.

'But you—' she began.

'I'm not on duty tomorrow—well, today,' he cut in. 'I'm awake now, too. And we can both catch up on our sleep later when the baby sleeps.'

'Are you sure?'

'Sure. Let's keep the light low for her, so she can sleep and we can see her.'

His duvet was still thrown over her sofa. 'Here—you might as well share the duvet with me,' he said, and tucked it over her. 'Try not to worry. We know it's not a bacterial infection, which is the important thing. Maybe it's the beginnings of a cold. Small babies tend to get temperature spikes when they get a cold. One minute they're fine, the next minute they're ill enough to worry the life out of you, and then they're absolutely fine again.' He took her hand. 'She's going to be perfectly all right, Amy. We're here and we're keeping an eye on her. And, before you say it, I'm used to not getting massive amounts of sleep. It comes with the job.'

'I guess,' she said. He was still holding her hand, and it made her feel better. She didn't pull away.

Amy woke, feeling groggy, to the sound of Hope crying.

When had she fallen asleep? How could she have neglected Hope like that? Guilt flooded through her.

But a crying baby was a good sign, right?

'OK?' Josh asked next to her, sounding much more awake than she felt.

'OK. My turn to sort her out,' she mumbled. Why had she thought it was a good idea to sit up all night on the sofa? She had a crick in her neck and her back ached. Right now she wasn't going to be a lot of use to the baby.

'It ought to be my turn,' he said, 'because she's due some more paracetamol.' He paused. 'They weighed her at hospital. Can you remember how much they said she weighed?'

'I didn't even register it,' she said. 'I was so worried that they were going to find something seriously wrong.'

'It's gone clean out of my head, too.' He blew out a breath. 'I don't want to guess at her weight and estimate the dose of paracetamol, so we're going to have to weigh her.'

'I don't actually own a pair of bathroom scales,' Amy admitted.

'How about kitchen scales, and a tray we can put her on for a moment?' Josh suggested.

She snapped the light on and gave him a wry smile. 'This has to be the strangest Boxing Day morning I've ever spent.'

'Me, too,' he said.

But at the same time it was a morning that filled her with relief—even more than the first night they'd spent with Hope, because now she knew that with Josh by her side she could face anything life threw at her.

'Give her a cuddle and I'll get the scales out,' she said.

She put a soft cloth on a baking tray, then put it on her kitchen scales and set them to zero. 'All righty.'

He set Hope on the tray and Amy peered at the display on the scales. 'Five pounds, ten ounces—or do you need it in metric?'

'Pounds and ounces are fine,' he said. 'I know how much infant paracetamol to give her now.'

He measured a dose of medicine for the baby and gave it to her through the oral syringe while Amy heated the milk.

'Sofa?' he asked.

She nodded and he carried Hope back to the sofa. This time, after he'd transferred the baby into Amy's arms so she could feed the baby, he slid one arm round Amy's shoulder.

It felt too nice for her to protest; right at that moment she felt warm, comforted and safe. After the scare that had taken them to the hospital, this was exactly what she needed. Maybe it was what he needed, too, she thought, and she tried not to overthink it. Or to start hoping that this meant Josh was starting to see her as more than just a neighbour. Yes, they could be friends. But on New Year's Day they'd have to give Hope back to the social worker—and when that part of their lives came to an end, what would happen?

Once the baby had finished drinking her milk—all sixty millilitres of it—Amy put her back in the Moses basket. Without comment, Josh put his arm round her shoulders again. Although part of Amy knew that she ought to put some distance between them, she couldn't help leaning into him, enjoying the feel of his muscular body against hers and his warmth.

They kept watch on the baby with the light turned down low, but finally Amy drifted back to sleep.

The next time Hope woke, it was a more reasonable time. Josh fed the baby while Amy showered and washed her hair, and then she took over baby duties while Josh went next door to shower and change.

She put cereals, yoghurt, jam and butter on the table, placed the bread next to the toaster, and while she waited for the kettle to boil she texted Jane Richards, the social worker.

Hope doing well. Had a bit of a temperature in the middle of the night but we checked her out at hospital and all OK. We have a theory about her mum: might be a girl from my class, but no proof. How do we check it out?

When she'd sent the text, she suddenly realised that she hadn't signed it. From the context, she was pretty sure that Jane would probably be able to work out who the text was from, but she sent a second text anyway.

This is Amy Howes btw. Not enough coffee or sleep! :)

Josh was back in her flat and they'd just finished breakfast when his phone rang.

'Do you mind if I get that?' he asked.

She spread her hands. 'It's fine.'

He returned with a smile. 'Remember Alison, the doctor who saw us last night?'

'Yes.'

'She's bringing us a pram and a snowsuit. She'll call me when she's parked and I'll go and let her in.'

Amy blinked. 'A pram and a snowsuit?'

'I'll let her explain. She's about twenty minutes away.'

True to her word, Alison called him to say that she'd just parked and had all the stuff with her.

'Feel free to ask her up for coffee,' Amy said as he headed for the door. 'It's the least I can do.'

'Thanks.'

He returned with Alison, carrying a pram, and Amy sorted out the hot drinks.

'Thank you so much for lending us the pram and snowsuit,' Amy said.

'No problem.' Alison smiled at her. 'I didn't think about it until after you'd left, but my sister was about to put her pram on eBay—it's one of those with a car seat that clips to the chassis to make a pram. She's happy to lend it to you while you're looking after Hope. And her youngest was tiny, so I've got some tiny baby clothes and a snowsuit as well. At least then you can take her out and all get some fresh air.'

'That's so kind,' Amy said.

'She didn't take much persuading,' Alison said. 'In situations like this, you always think how easily it could have been you or someone close to you. Poor little love. How's she doing?'

'Her temperature's gone down—but, when we had to give her more paracetamol this morning, I forgot how much she weighed,' Josh admitted.

'So poor little Hope had to lie on a towel on a baking tray, so we could weigh her on my kitchen scales,' Amy added.

Alison laughed. 'I can just imagine it. And, tsk, Josh, you being a consultant and forgetting something as important as a baby's weight.'

'I know. I'm totally hanging my head in shame,' Josh said, looking anything but repentant.

Amy suddenly had a very clear idea of what he was like to work with—as nice as he was as a neighbour, kind and good-humoured and compassionate, yet strong when it was necessary. Given his gorgeous blue eyes and the way his hair seemed to be messy again five minutes after he'd combed it, she'd just bet that half the female staff at the hospital had a crush on him. Not that he'd notice. Josh wasn't full of himself and aware of his good looks, the way Gavin and even Michael had been. He was genuine.

And he was off limits, she reminded herself.

Alison peered into the Moses basket. 'She's a little cutie.'

'Pick her up and give her a cuddle, if you like,' Amy said.

Alison smiled, needing no second invitation. 'I love babies. Especially when I can give them back when it comes to nappy changes.'

'Noted,' Josh said dryly.

'So she was just left in the lobby in your flats?' Alison asked.

'Yes.' Amy ran through what had happened. 'And we have a theory that her mum might be in my form group.'

'But if the mum's in your class, Amy, how come you didn't recognise her handwriting?' Alison asked.

'Because she's in my form group, not my class. I don't teach her,' Amy explained. 'It means she's there in the form room for five minutes in the morning for registration, and twenty minutes in the afternoon for registration and whatever other activities we're doing in form time—giving out letters for parents, a chance for any of them to talk to me if they're worried about something, and sometimes we do quizzes and the kind of things that help the kids bond a bit. I never see any of her written work. And it's still only a theory. If we're wrong, then we still have no clue who Hope's mum is.'

'Well, I hope they do find the poor little mite's mum.' Alison looked at Josh. 'So you two are sort of living together this week?'

'As friends,' Josh said swiftly. 'It makes sense, because otherwise we'd have to keep transferring the baby between flats and it'd unsettle her.'

Amy reminded herself that they weren't a couple. Even if they had slept on the sofa together last night and fallen asleep holding hands, and when he'd put his arm round her it had simply been comfort for both of them after their worry about the baby's health.

'It's really nice of you to look after her,' Alison said.

'What else could we do?' Amy asked. 'She's a baby. She didn't ask to be left here. The social worker couldn't get a placement because it was Christmas Eve and nobody was about, and Josh said the hospital's on black alert so the baby couldn't stay there.'

'The winter vomiting virus is everywhere,' Alison confirmed, 'and the children's ward is full of babies with bronchiolitis, something you definitely don't want a newborn to get.' She smiled at them, then handed the baby back to Amy. 'Here you go, cutie. Back to your Aunty Amy. Thanks for the coffee and biscuits. I'm heading home to bed now because I'm working the night shift again tonight and I need some sleep before I face the fractures and the ones who gave themselves food poisoning with the leftovers.'

'Thanks for bringing all this,' Josh said, 'and I owe your sister flowers and some decent chocolate. And you, too.'

Alison waved away the thanks. 'It's good to be able to do something nice for someone at Christmas. It feels as if it's putting the balance back a bit, after all the greed and rampant consumerism.'

When she'd gone, Josh turned to Amy. 'The only time you've been out of the flat since Christmas Eve morning is our middle-of-the-night trip to hospital. Do you want to go and get some fresh air?'

'That'd be good. And I could probably do with picking up something for dinner,' she said. 'I forgot to get something out of the freezer earlier.'

'I ought to be the one buying dinner,' he said. 'You've fed me two days running as it is.'

'It really doesn't matter.' Unable to resist teasing him, she added, 'But if you really want to cook for me…'

'Then you get a choice of spaghetti Bolognese or a cheese toastie,' he said promptly.

'Or maybe I should teach you how to cook something else.' She grabbed her coat and her handbag. 'I'll see you in a bit. I've got my phone with me in case you need me.'

'Great.'

It felt odd, being alone in Amy's flat, Josh thought when she'd gone. Weirdly, it felt like home; yet, at the same time, it wasn't. Everything was neat and tidy and she'd done the washing up while he was seeing Alison out of the flat, so he couldn't do anything practical to help; all he could really do was watch the baby.

He'd texted his parents and his siblings during his break at work on Christmas Day, and hadn't corrected their assumption that he was working today. Not that he really wanted to speak to any of them. If he told them how his Christmas had panned out, he knew they'd try to manage it—which drove him crazy. He was perfectly capable of managing his own life, even if he was the baby of the family and had messed up, in their eyes.

He held the baby and looked at the framed photographs on Amy's mantelpiece. The older couple were clearly her parents, and the man in one of the younger couples looked enough like her to be her brother in Canada. The other couple, he assumed, must be the friends she'd talked about staying with in Edinburgh.

'She really loves her family,' he said to the baby, 'and they clearly love her to bits, too.' He sighed. 'Maybe I should make more of an effort with mine.'

The baby gurgled, as if agreeing.

'They're not bad people. Just they have set views on what I ought to be doing with my life, and right now they feel I'm letting them down. I'm the only one in our family to get divorced. But Kelly didn't love me any more, and I couldn't expect her to stay with me just to keep my family happy. It would have made both of us really miserable, and that's not fair.'

The baby gurgled again.

'Tell you a secret,' he said. 'I think I could like Amy. More than like her.'

The baby cooed, as if to say that she liked Amy, too.

'And I would never have got to know her like this if it wasn't for you, Munchkin. We'd still just be doing the nod-and-smile thing if we saw each other in the corridor or the lobby. But this last couple of days, I've spent more time with her than I have with anyone else in a long, long time.' He paused. 'The question is, what does she think about me?'

The baby was silent.

'I'm not going to risk making things awkward while we're looking after you,' he said. 'But in the New Year I'm going to ask her out properly. Because I'm ready to move on, and I think she might be, too.'

* * *

It felt odd being out of the flat, Amy thought. It was nice to get some fresh air, but at the same time she found she couldn't stop thinking about Hope.

Or about Josh.

But what did she have to offer him?

If he wanted to settle down and have a family, then it couldn't be with her. She knew that there were other ways of having a child as well as biologically, but Michael had refused flat-out even to consider fostering or adoption. She wondered how he would've reacted to Hope; she had a nasty feeling that he would've decided it wasn't his problem and would've left it to the authorities.

Josh, on the other hand, had real compassion. He'd been instantly supportive. Even though he didn't know her well, he'd offered help when it was needed most.

She shook herself. She and Josh were neighbours, making their way towards becoming good friends. Their relationship couldn't be any more than that, so she would have to be sensible about this and damp down her burgeoning feelings towards him.

The supermarket was crowded with people looking for post-Christmas bargains. Amy avoided the clearance shelves and headed for the chiller cabinet. A few minutes later, she paid for her groceries at the checkout, and went back to the flat.

'You're back early,' he said.

'The shops were heaving.' And it hadn't felt right to go to the park without the baby. Which she knew was crazy, because Hope wasn't hers and would only be here for a couple more days. 'I thought we'd have French bread, cheese and chutney for lunch.'

'Sounds perfect. I'll prepare it, if you like, while you give our girl a cuddle.'

Her gaze met his and her heart felt as if it had just done a somersault.

'Temporary girl,' he corrected himself swiftly.

'I know what you meant.' Being with Josh and Hope felt like being part of a new family. It was so tempting, but she mustn't let herself forget that it was only temporary. Clearly Josh felt the same way. If only things were a little different. If only she'd never met Gavin, or had at least been a bit less clueless, so she'd been able to get the chlamydia treated in time...

But things were as they were, and she'd have to make the best of it instead of whining for something she knew wasn't going to happen.

'Did Jane reply to your text?' he asked.

'Not yet. And it wasn't an emergency, so I'm not expecting her to pick it up until at least tomorrow.'

'You're probably right,' he said. 'Hope's temperature has come down a lot, but it's probably too much for her to go out for a stroll in the park.' There was a definite wistfulness in his expression as he glanced at the pram.

'Maybe tomorrow,' she said.

After lunch, they spent the afternoon playing board games. 'I haven't done this for a while, either,' she admitted ruefully. 'I'd forgotten how much fun it is.'

'Remember what you said to me,' he said. 'Make the time for stuff you enjoy.'

Josh sketched Hope again in the back of the notebook after her next feed, and couldn't resist making a sneaky sketch of Amy. Though in a way that was a bad idea, because it made him really aware of the curve of her mouth and the way her hair fell—and it made him want to touch her.

He still couldn't shake how it had felt this morning to draw her into his arms and hold her close. OK, so they'd both been dog-tired and in need of comfort after their worry about Hope and a very broken night—but it had felt so right to hold her like that and fall asleep with her on the sofa.

For Hope's sake, he needed to rein himself back a bit.

'While Madam's asleep,' Amy said, thankfully oblivious to what he'd been thinking, 'maybe I can teach you how to cook something really simple and really impressive.'

'Which is?' he asked.

'Baked salmon with sweet chilli sauce, served with mangetout and crushed new potatoes.'

It sounded complicated. But clearly Amy was good at her day job, because she gave him really clear instructions and talked him through making dinner.

'I can't believe I made this,' he said, looking at the plates. After the first mouthful, he amended that to, 'I *really* can't believe I made this.'

'Healthy and impressive,' she said. 'And it's easy. Josh, what you do at work every day is way harder than cooking dinner.'

'Maybe.' But cooking for one was no fun. Which was the main reason why he lived on toasted sandwiches and takeaways.

They spent the evening curled up on the sofa, watching films. Josh was careful this time not to give in to the temptation of holding Amy's hand or drawing her into his arms.

But, after Hope's last feed of the evening, he could see the worry on Amy's face.

'Maybe we should both sleep on the sofa again tonight,' he said. 'We can still take turns at getting up for her, but it also means if you're worried you can wake me more quickly.'

She took a deep breath. 'Don't take this the wrong way,' she said, 'but I was thinking along the same lines. My bed's a double and it'll be a lot more comfortable than the sofa. We're adults and we can share a bed without...'

His mouth went dry as he finished the sentence mentally. *Without making love.*

Which was what he really wanted to do with Amy. Kiss her, discover where she liked being touched and what made her eyes go dark with pleasure.

'Fully dressed,' he said. Because lying in bed with her, with them both wearing pyjamas, might be a little too much temptation for him to resist. And he hoped she couldn't hear the slight huskiness in his voice.

'Of course.'

Her bedroom was exactly as he'd expected, all soft creams and feminine, yet without being frilly or fussy and over the top. There was a framed picture of a seascape on the wall, the curtains were floral chintz, and the whole room was restful and peaceful.

Though when he lay next to her in bed with the light off—with both of them fully dressed—he was far from feeling restful and peaceful. He was too aware of the last time he'd shared a bed with someone, just over a year ago. OK, so he'd finally got to the stage where he could move on with his life… But could it be with Amy? He definitely had feelings for her, and he was fairly sure that it was mutual; but was it because they'd had this intense sharing of space over the last few days, while they'd been looking after Hope, or was it something real? Would he be enough for her, the way he hadn't been for Kelly? Or would everything between them change again at New Year, once the baby had gone?

When Hope cried, Amy got out of bed on autopilot and scooped the baby from the Moses basket. As she padded into the kitchen with the baby in her arms, she woke up fully. Was it her imagination, or did Hope feel hot again?

And then Hope only took half her usual amount of milk.

Panic welled through her, and she switched on her bedside light on its lowest setting. 'Josh.'

He woke immediately and sat up. 'What's wrong?'

'I might be being paranoid, but she didn't take that much milk just now, and I think she's hot again.'

He checked the baby over, then grabbed the thermometer and took her temperature. 'Her temperature's normal.'

'So I'm just being ridiculous.'

He settled the baby back into the Moses basket. 'No. You're being completely normal. I'd worry, too.' He wrapped his arms round her. 'You're doing just fine, Amy.'

For someone who was never going to be a mum?

She wasn't sure what made her lean into him—the worry that had made her knees sag, or just the fact that he was there, holding her and seeming to infuse his strength into her as he kept his arms round her.

And was that his mouth against her cheek, in a reassuring kiss?

Something made her tip her head back.

The next thing she knew, his mouth was against hers. Soft, reassuring, gentle.

And then it wasn't like that any more, because somehow her mouth had opened beneath his and her arms were wrapped round his neck, and he was holding her much more tightly. And the warmth turned to heat, to sheer molten desire.

Then he pulled back.

Oh, God. How embarrassing was she? Throwing herself at her neighbour. Pathetic.

'Sorry,' she mumbled, hanging her head and unable to meet his eyes. Hot shame bubbled through her. What the hell had she just done?

'I should be the one apologising to you.'

Because he'd been kind? Because he'd stopped before she'd *really* made a fool of herself?

'No,' she muttered, still not wanting to look at him and see the pity in his face.

'Maybe I should sleep on your sofa again,' he said.

And then things would be even more awkward between them in the morning. 'No, it's fine. We're neighbours—*friends*—and we're adults; and we both need to be here for Hope.' She took a deep breath. 'We can both pretend that just now didn't happen.'

'Good idea,' he said.

But she still couldn't face him when she climbed into bed and switched off the light. And she noticed that there was a very large gap in the bed between them, as if he felt as uncomfortable and embarrassed about the situation as she did.

If only she'd kept that iron control she'd prided herself on so much before today. If only she hadn't kissed him. If only she hadn't given in to temptation.

She'd just have to hope that the broken night would affect his memory and he'd forget everything about what had just happened.

And she'd really have to put out of her mind how good it had felt in those moments when he'd kissed her back.

CHAPTER SIX

Bank Holiday Monday

AMY WAS WARM and deeply, deeply comfortable.

And then she realised why.

Somehow, during the night, the large gap in the bed between her and Josh had closed. Now her head was pillowed on his shoulder, his arm was round her shoulders, her arm was wrapped round his waist, and her fingers were twined with his.

They were sleeping like lovers.

Oh, help. This was a seriously bad idea. She couldn't offer Josh a future and it wasn't fair to lead him on.

Gently, she disentangled her fingers from his. She'd just started to wriggle quietly out of his arms, hoping she wouldn't wake him, when he said, 'Good morning.'

No running away from the situation, then. They were going to have to face this head on.

'Good morning,' she muttered. 'I—um—sorry about this.'

'Me, too.' Though he didn't sound concerned or embarrassed.

'I—um—we're both tired and sleep-deprived,' she said. 'And I guess this was bound to happen as we're sharing a bed. Propinquity and all that. It doesn't mean we have...' She paused, looking for the right word. 'Intentions.'

'Absolutely,' he agreed.

Was he smiling?

She didn't dare look.

'I'll go and make us a cup of tea before Hope wakes,' she said, and wriggled out of his arms properly.

She splashed her face with cold water in the bathroom, in the hope that it would bring back her common sense. It didn't. She could still feel the warmth of Josh's arms around her, and she wanted more. So much more.

How selfish could she get?

Cross with her own stupidity, she filled the kettle with water and rummaged in the cupboard for the tea bags.

Waking with Amy in his arms was just what Josh had been dreaming about. It had taken him a moment to realise that he was awake, and she really *was* in his arms.

She'd blamed it on them both being tired and sleep-deprived, and the fact that they'd slept in the same bed. But she'd sounded distinctly flustered.

So did she feel the same way about him that he was starting to feel about her?

He'd promised himself that he'd hold back from starting a relationship with her until after the baby was settled—either with her birth mother, or with long-term foster parents. But they'd kissed, last night. They'd woken in each other's arms, as if they were meant to be there. He'd been awake before Amy and she'd stayed in his arms for a few moments after she'd woken—which she wouldn't have done if she hadn't wanted to be there.

So maybe he needed to be brave and tell her what was in his head, and see if she felt the same way.

He climbed out of bed, checked that Hope was still asleep and not overheated, and then walked into the kitchen. Amy was making the tea, dressed in rumpled clothes and with her hair all over the place—and she'd never looked more beautiful to him or more natural.

'Hey.' He walked over to her and wrapped his arms round her. 'I know I probably shouldn't be doing this, and we don't know each other very well, but we've spent a lot of time together over the last couple of days and I really like you.' He paused. 'And I think you might like me too.'

This was the moment where either she would push him away in utter shock and he'd have to avoid her for the next six months until things were back on an even keel between them, or she would tell him that she felt the same.

He really hoped it was going to be the latter.

But then an expression of pure misery crossed her face and she stepped back out of his embrace. 'I do like you,' she admitted, 'but we can't do this.'

'Because of the baby?'

She took a deep breath. 'No, not because of her.'

'Then why?' Josh asked, not understanding.

'I need to tell you something about myself.' She finished making the mugs of tea, and handed one to him. 'Let's go and sit down.'

'This sounds serious.'

'It is,' she said grimly, 'and there isn't an easy way to say it, so I'm not going to sugar-coat it.'

He followed her into the living room. She sat down at one end of the sofa; he sat next to her, wondering just what kind of bombshell she was about to drop. Was she still married to her ex? No, she couldn't be—hadn't she said something about him getting married to someone else and expecting a baby now? So what kind of thing would hold her back from starting a new relationship?

He could see her eyes fill with tears. Whatever it was, it was something really serious. Something that hurt her. And he ached for her.

Finally, she said, her voice sounding broken, 'I can't have children.'

Josh wanted to reach out and take her hand and tell her that it didn't change the way he felt, but he could see the 'hands off' signals written all over her. And as a doctor he knew the value of silence. If he let her talk, tell him exactly what was holding her back, then he might have more of a chance of being able to counter her arguments.

'That's why Michael—my ex—broke off our engagement and left,' she continued.

Josh was horrified. It must've been hard enough for Amy, finding out that she couldn't have children, but then for the man who was supposed to love her and want to marry her to walk out on her over the issue... That shocked him to the core. How could Michael have been so selfish? Why hadn't he put Amy first? And how it must've hurt her when she'd learned that his new wife was expecting a baby.

'We'd been trying for a baby for a year or so without success, so we went for investigations to find out why we couldn't conceive.' She looked away. 'I knew that the guy I'd dated before Michael had cheated on me. I found it had been more than once and with more than one other woman, and that's why I left him. I didn't want to stay with someone who didn't love me or respect me enough to be faithful. But what I didn't realise was that he'd given me chlamydia.'

Josh knew then exactly what had happened to her. 'You didn't have any symptoms?'

She shook her head. 'And obviously, because I didn't know I had it, that meant I was still infected when I started seeing Michael and we moved in together. I infected Michael. He didn't have symptoms, either.'

Quite a high percentage of people who'd been infected with chlamydia didn't have symptoms. Not that it would comfort her to know that. 'Amy, it wasn't your fault.'

She shook her head. 'I should've been more careful. Used condoms with Gavin—the one who cheated on me—instead of the Pill.'

How could she possibly blame herself? 'Before you found out that he'd cheated on you, you trusted him. How long were you together?'

'Two years.'

'So of course you'd think the Pill was a safe form of contraception. Any woman in your shoes would.' Josh shook his head, angry on her behalf. 'Gavin cheated on you, and he was the one who infected you. How could anyone possibly think it was your fault?'

'Because I should've got myself checked out. I should've realised that, because Gavin had been sleeping around, there could be consequences.'

'But you didn't have symptoms. Actually, around two thirds of women and about fifty per cent of men don't have symptoms if they're infected with chlamydia. And, if you don't have symptoms, how are you supposed to know there's a problem? It's *not* your fault,' he said again. 'I'm probably speaking out of turn, but it was totally unfair of Michael to blame you.'

'It happened. And you can't change the past, just learn from it.' She shrugged. 'So now you know. As a doctor, you've probably already guessed what the problem is, but I'll spell it out for you. The chlamydia gave me pelvic inflammatory disease and the scar tissue blocked my Fallopian tubes, so I can't have children. If you're looking to have a family in the future, then I'm not the one for you and we need to call a halt to this right now.'

And that was really what was holding her back? This time, he did reach over and take her hand. 'First of all, having children isn't the be-all and end-all of a relationship. Lots of couples can't have children or choose not to. It doesn't make their relationship and how they feel about each other any less valid. And if this thing between us works out the way I hope it might, then if we do decide in the future that we want children then we still have options. Did your specialist not mention IVF?'

She swallowed. 'Yes, but Michael didn't want to do that.'

Josh wasn't surprised. And he'd just bet the other man's reasoning was purely to do with himself, not to do with how tough the IVF process could be for a woman.

'It's not an easy option and there are no cast-iron guarantees,' he said, 'but it's still an option for tubal infertility. One of the doctors I trained with had severe endometriosis which blocked her Fallopian tubes, and she had a baby through IVF last year.'

Was that hope he saw flickering in her eyes, just then?

'And if that's not a route you want to go down—because the treatment cycle is pretty gruelling and it isn't for everyone—there's fostering or adoption.'

She blinked, as if not expecting him to have reacted that way. 'Michael wasn't prepared to even consider that.'

Because Michael was a selfish toad. Not that it was Josh's place to say so. 'I'm not Michael,' he said.

'I know.' She took a deep breath. 'But I wanted you to know the situation upfront. So, if it's a problem for you, you can walk away now and there's no damage to either of us.'

Even though they'd only got close to each other over the last couple of days, Josh had the strongest feeling that walking away from her would definitely cause damage to both of them.

'I like you,' he said again, 'and I think you might just like me back. And that's what's important here. Everything else is just details and we can work them out. Together.'

She looked at him as if she didn't quite believe him.

'If you want to work them out, that is,' he said. 'Your infertility doesn't make any difference to the way I feel about you. I still want to start dating you properly. Get to know you.'

'And it's really that easy?'

'It is for me.' He paused. 'Though, since you told me about your ex, I guess you need to know about mine.'

* * *

The woman who'd left him last Christmas Eve, pregnant with another man's child.

Amy really couldn't understand why on earth anyone would dump a man like Josh—a man who was kind and caring as well as easy on the eye. In the intense couple of days they'd spent together, she hadn't found a deal-breaking flaw in him.

'Kelly worked in advertising—so maybe if I'd gone to art college instead of med school we would've ended up working together.' He shrugged. 'But we met at a party, where we were both a friend of a friend. We fell for each other, moved in together a couple of weeks later and got married within three months.'

Alarm bells rang in the back of Amy's head. Wasn't this exactly what she and Josh were doing? Falling in love with each other a little too quickly and not thinking things through? A whirlwind romance had gone badly wrong for him before. Then again, her last two relationships had both lasted for a couple of years, so taking things slowly hadn't exactly worked for her, either.

'I assumed Kelly would want a family at some point in the future, the way I did, and she assumed that we were both ambitious and were going to put our careers first,' he said. 'We probably should have talked about that a lot more before we got married.'

He wanted a family.

Amy's heart sank.

OK, he'd said to her that her infertility didn't make a difference. But it did. As he'd said, IVF treatment could be gruelling and there were no guarantees that it would work. She'd looked into it, in the days when she'd still hoped that Michael might change his mind, and the chances of having a baby were roughly one in four. Odds which might not be good enough for Josh. Right now, they were looking after a baby together. What would happen in New Year, when life went back to normal? Would he realise then what a mistake he was making, trying to make a go of things with her?

'Kelly was working really long hours on the promise of getting a promotion. Obviously I supported her,' Josh continued, 'but then she fell in love with one of her colleagues. She said they tried to fight the attraction; but, on one project they were working on together, they went to visit a client and it meant an overnight stay. They were in rooms next to each other in the hotel; they'd had dinner out with the client and too much wine; and one thing led to another. That's when the affair started.'

Clearly Josh hadn't had a clue about it. Amy reached over and squeezed his hand. 'That's hard.'

'Yeah.' He sighed. 'She got the promotion, but she was still working crazy hours. I assumed it was because of the pressure of work in her new job, but it was actually because she was seeing the other guy.' He gave her a wry smile. 'Then she told me she was pregnant.'

'And you thought it was yours?'

'I knew it wasn't,' he said softly, 'because we'd both been working mad hours and were too tired to do anything more than fall into bed and go straight to sleep when we got home at night. We hadn't had sex for a couple of months, so there was no way the baby could possibly be mine. Though Kelly never lied to me about it. She told me it was his and she was sorry— she'd fallen in love with him and was leaving me.' He looked away. 'Funny, she ended up with the family she said she didn't want, but maybe it was really that she just didn't want to have a family with me. I wasn't enough for her.'

How could Josh possibly not be enough for someone? Amy squeezed his hand again. 'Josh, you didn't do anything wrong. It wasn't your fault.' She gave him an awkward smile. 'I guess you can't help who you fall in love with.' Hadn't she made that same mistake, falling for Mr Wrong?

'And Kelly was fair about it. She didn't try to heap the blame on me for the divorce.'

'Even when the split's amicable, it's still tough,' Amy said. 'I'm sorry you got hurt like that.'

'But?' he asked, clearly sensing that she had doubts.

'But,' she said softly, 'you said you wanted to have a family with Kelly. Even if we put IVF into the equation, there's still a very strong chance I won't be able to give you a family. So I'll understand if you want us to stay just friends.'

He shook his head. 'I want more than that from you, Amy. And in any relationship you have to make a compromise.'

'But this is one hell of a compromise. It means giving up on your plans to have a family.'

'Right now, it's still early days between you and me, and we're not making any promises to each other of happy ever after,' he said. 'But I really like you, Amy, and if it's a choice of being with you and looking at alternatives for having a family, or not being with you, then I'm on the side of alternatives.' He smiled at her. 'And we're not doing so badly with Hope. I'm beginning to think that her mum gave her exactly the right name, and also that you were right because the baby's giving us the Christmas we both need. She's brought us together and she's giving us a chance to find happiness again—together.'

Amy thought about it. 'Yes,' she said.

'So, you and me. No pressure. We'll see where things take us.'

'Sounds good to me,' Amy said. And it felt as if spring flowers had just pushed through the ground to brighten up the days after a long, long winter.

Just before lunch, Jane the social worker rang. 'How's the baby doing?' she asked.

'Fine,' Amy said. 'She's still got a bit of a temperature, but it's going down.'

'Good. So what's this theory you've got about the baby's mum?'

'Hang on—let me put you on speaker phone so Josh can hear as well and chip in,' Amy said. 'We think she might be a girl in my form. I didn't recognise the handwriting on the note because I don't actually teach her, so there's no reason for me ever to see her work or her writing.'

'We did think about maybe going round to see her for a chat,' Josh said.

'No—it's better to leave this to the authorities,' Jane said, 'especially if you don't have any proof that it's definitely her. What makes you think it's her, Amy?'

'She's gone very quiet, lately. I did bring it up with her mum, who said it was because her new partner had moved in and Freya was having trouble adjusting to the idea of someone she saw trying to take her dad's place.' She paused. 'Freya wears quite baggy clothes, not skinny trousers or anything. And because it's winter it's easier to hide a pregnancy under a baggy sweater.'

'Does she look as if she's put on weight?'

'A little bit, but body image is a really sensitive area for teens, and I guessed she might be comfort-eating if she wasn't happy at home,' Amy said. 'Drawing attention to it would only have made her feel worse, and the last thing I wanted was for her to start starving herself or taking diet pills. I was going to have a chat with her in the New Year.' She paused. 'I thought that might be why she kept rushing to the loo.'

'But that's also a symptom of late pregnancy,' Josh said.

'So how do we tackle this?' Amy asked.

'You don't. I do it,' Jane said. 'Under the safeguarding rules, Amy, I know you can give me the contact information of a student you're worried about, so can you tell me her name and address?'

Amy had accessed Freya's school records earlier, and gave Jane the relevant details.

'Thanks. I'll liaise with the police, then do a preliminary visit and see if I can get any information,' Jane said. 'And thank you.'

'Will you let me know how you get on?' Amy asked.

'I'm afraid any conversations I have will be confidential, unless I have Freya's permission to talk to you,' Jane said, sounding regretful.

'We understand. But please tell her from us that the baby's doing just fine and we'd be happy to send her a picture, or for her to come and visit Hope,' Josh said. 'And if she does turn out to be our missing mum, please persuade her to see a doctor to get checked over.

She won't be in trouble, but we need to be sure that she's all right.'

'I will,' Jane promised.

Amy looked at Josh when she'd ended the call. 'I really hope we've done the right thing.'

'We have,' he said. 'Jane's in a neutral position so, if our theory's wrong, then Freya won't be too embarrassed to walk into your form room next term. If it's right, then Jane knows all the procedures and can get Freya the help she needs.'

'I'd still rather go and see her myself,' Amy said. 'As you say, Jane's neutral and she's really nice, but she's still a stranger. Surely Freya's more likely to open up to me because she knows me?'

'If our theory's right, Freya left Hope with you because she trusted you to do the right thing and talk to the right people for her. Which you've done,' Josh pointed out.

'I guess.'

Hope woke; as soon as Amy picked her up, she could tell what the problem was. 'Nappy. Super-bad nappy,' she said.

'Oh, great,' Josh said with a sigh. 'And it's my turn to change her.'

'I'm not arguing.' Amy smiled and handed the baby over. Josh carried Hope to the bathroom. 'Come on, Munchkin. Let's sort you out.'

Josh was gone a very long time. And Amy could hear screaming, interspersed with him singing snatches of what sounded like every song that came into his head. Each one sounded slightly more desperate.

She was just about to go and see if she could do

anything to help when he came back into the kitchen carrying a red-faced, still grizzly baby.

'I was just about to come and see if you needed anything. Do I take it that it was really bad?' she asked.

'Let's just say she needed a bath,' he said grimly. 'And she doesn't like baths yet.'

'Hence the screaming and the singing?'

'Yeah.' He blew out a breath. 'I'm glad I'm not a teenager. After that nightmare in the bathroom just now, I'd be paranoid that my face was all it took to make any girl scream and run away.'

Amy couldn't help laughing. 'Hardly. You're quite pretty.'

'Pretty?' He gave her a speaking look.

'If you were a supply teacher at my school,' she said, 'you'd have gaggles of teenage girls hanging around the staff room every lunchtime in the hope of catching a glimpse of you.'

'That,' he said, 'sounds scary. I think I'd rather deal with—wait for it...' He adopted a pose and warbled to the tune of 'The Twelve Days of Christmas'. 'Five turkey carvers! Four black eyes, three throwing up, two broken ankles and a bead up a toddler's nose.'

'I ought to introduce you to our head of music,' she said, laughing. 'Between you, I can imagine you writing a panto about *The Twelve Days of ED*.'

'Better believe it.'

'So, what do you want to do this afternoon?'

'It's wet and miserable out there, and although Hope's on the mend I'd rather not take her out, even though we've got the pram and snowsuit,' Josh said.

'Festive films on the sofa, then,' she said.

He wrinkled his nose. 'I feel a bit guilty, just slob-bing around on the sofa.'

'As you said, it's not the weather for going out,' she reminded him. 'And you've had tough enough shifts to justify doing nothing for a day or so. Well, nothing but alternate feeds, changing the odd really vile nappy and singing songs to stop Hope crying.'

'Well, if you put it that way…' He stole a kiss. 'Bring on the films.'

Snuggled up on the sofa with Josh and the baby, Amy had never felt more at peace. What had started off as a miserable Christmas was rapidly turning into one of the best Christmases ever.

'Do you want me to take the sofa tonight?' he asked when Hope had had her late evening feed.

'I think we go for the same deal as last night,' Amy said. 'Except maybe this time we could change into pyjamas instead of sleeping in our clothes?'

'Give me two minutes next door,' he said.

And she burst out laughing when he returned in a pair of pyjamas covered in Christmas puddings. 'That's priceless. I'm almost tempted to take a snap of you wearing them and put it in Hope's book.'

'Absolutely not. These were my best friend's wife's idea of a joke,' he said. 'I don't usually wear pyjamas. When they stayed at my flat after my housewarm-ing, I ended up wearing a ratty old T-shirt and a pair of boxer shorts so I'd be decent, and she said I needed proper pyjamas for when I had guests. This is the only pair I own. And this is the first time I've worn them.'

Amy went hot all over at the thought of Josh, in bed with her, naked. All the words flew out of her head and she just said, flustered, 'I, um…'

He took her hand and kissed the back of each finger in turn, then turned her hand over and pressed a kiss into the palm. 'Don't be flustered. There's no pressure,' he said, his voice low and husky and sexy as anything. 'Let's go to bed. Platonically.'

And he was as good as his word. No pressure. He simply curled his body round hers, wrapped his arm round her waist, and rested his cheek against her shoulder. And, as she fell asleep, Amy felt happier than she'd been in a long, long while.

CHAPTER SEVEN

Tuesday

ON TUESDAY MORNING, Josh woke to find his arms wrapped round Amy and hers wrapped round him. And suddenly the whole world felt full of promise. He couldn't resist kissing her awake. To his relief, she didn't back away from him the way she had the previous morning; this time, she smiled and kissed him back.

'Well, happy Tuesday,' he said.

She stroked his face. 'Absolutely.'

'My turn to bring you a cup of tea in bed,' he said, kissed her lingeringly and climbed out of bed.

'Wonderful,' she said, smiling back at him.

Funny, being in her kitchen was so much better than being in his own. Even though they had similar decor, all in neutral tones, her place felt like *home*. Josh even found himself humming a happy song as he made tea.

He could hear Hope crying, and called through, 'I'll heat up some milk for Munchkin.'

'Thanks,' Amy called back.

He took the two mugs of tea and bottle of milk through to Amy's bedroom, where he found Amy cuddling the baby and crooning to her. He set the tea on her bedside table and climbed back in next to them. 'Want me to feed her?'

'Sure.' Amy transferred the baby into his arms.

Feeding the baby, cuddled up next to Amy in bed… It made Josh realise exactly what he wanted out of life—what he wanted to happen in the New Year.

To be part of a family, just like this, with Amy. Domestic bliss.

Given her fertility issues, it wasn't going to be easy. But he thought it was going to be worth the effort. The only thing was: after they gave Hope back at New Year, would Amy change her mind about him?

Amy sipped her tea and watched Josh feeding the baby. This was exactly what she wanted. To be a family, with Josh. Although part of her was still worried that her infertility was going to be an issue, he'd been very clear about being happy to look at the options of IVF treatment, adoption or fostering. So maybe it wouldn't be an issue after all.

'She's drunk a bit more than usual, this morning,' Josh said. 'That's a good sign. Maybe we can take her out this morning.'

Amy went over to the window and peeked through the curtain. 'The sun's shining.'

'How about we go for lunch in the park?' he suggested.

'And we can try out Alison's sister's pram. Great idea.' She paused. 'How often are you supposed to weigh babies?'

'I don't know.' He smiled. 'Time for the baking tray again?'

'Hey. It was being inventive,' she protested, laughing. 'And it worked, didn't it?'

Once they'd showered and dressed, Amy changed Hope's nappy and they weighed her. 'Five pounds, twelve ounces.'

'We need to write that in her book,' Josh said, and did so while Amy got the baby dressed. Between them, they got her into the snowsuit.

'It dwarfs her,' he said ruefully.

'Better too big than too small,' Amy said.

'I guess.' Josh tucked the baby into the pram underneath a blanket, and then put the apron on the pram. 'Just in case it's a bit breezy out there,' he said.

'Good idea,' Amy agreed.

Once they'd got their own coats on, they negotiated the pram out of the flat.

'This is where I'm really glad we're on the ground floor,' Amy said.

'Me, too,' Josh said. 'Even though this pram's really light, it wouldn't be much fun carrying it up or down a flight of stairs—especially if you're doing it on your own.'

They exchanged a glance, and Amy knew that he too was thinking of Hope's mum. If she was given a flat in a high-rise block, it could be tough for her to cope.

'Let's go to the park,' she said firmly. 'This is your first official trip out, Hope.'

'We ought to commemorate that for Hope's book,' Josh said. 'Time for a selfie.'

'In the lobby?'

'With the pram. You bet.' He looked at her. 'Ready?'

They crouched either side of the pram, and Josh angled his phone so he could take the snap of the three of them together.

Hope slept all the way to the park. Meanwhile Josh slid his arm round Amy's shoulders, and they both had one hand on the handle of the pram, pushing it together.

This felt like being part of the family Amy had always wanted. She knew it was just a fantasy, and if the police couldn't find Hope's mother then the baby would go formally into care, but for now she was going to enjoy feeling this way.

The sun seemed to have brought out all the other new parents, Josh thought. People happily strolling along the paths, pushing prams, sometimes with a toddler in tow as well. Slightly older children were playing on the swings, slides and climbing frames in the park, while their parents chatted and kept an eye on them from benches placed around the perimeter of the play area.

Just for a moment he could imagine the three of them here in three years' time: himself pushing Hope on the swings as she laughed and begged to be pushed higher, while Amy stood watching them, her face radiant and her belly swollen with their new baby.

Except there were no guarantees that the IVF treatment would work, and the chances of them actually being able to keep Hope were minimal.

He knew he was being ridiculous. Right from the start, this had been a temporary arrangement; the baby was theirs only for a week, and that was simply because they were the neighbours who'd found her abandoned on their doorstep on a day where none of the official services were able to help. They couldn't be a family with Hope.

But maybe they could help another child, through fostering or adoption.

And he knew without doubt that Amy was the one he wanted to share that family with. Thanks to Hope, he'd found that he was finally ready to move on from the wreckage of his marriage to Kelly; and because he'd been cooped up with Amy for several days he'd had the chance to get to know her properly. He could actually be himself with Amy, and it was a long time since he'd felt that.

When they stopped for a coffee and a toasted sandwich in the café in the park, the pictures were still in his head, and he found himself sketching the scene on the back of a napkin.

If only this wasn't temporary.

But for now he was going to enjoy the Christmas break he'd expected to hate.

Later that afternoon, Amy was in the middle of feeding Hope when her intercom buzzed.

'Would you mind getting that?' she asked Josh.

'Sure.' He picked up the handset. 'Hello?'

'Is that Josh? It's Jane Richards.'

'Come in,' he said, and buzzed her in. 'It's Jane,' he said to Amy as he replaced the handset. 'I'll put the kettle on.'

Had Jane talked to Freya? And was their theory right? Or was Jane just checking up on them in their role as temporary foster parents?

Josh answered the door when Jane knocked. 'The kettle's just about to boil. Tea or coffee?'

'Tea would be wonderful, thanks,' she said.

'How do you like your tea?'

'Reasonably strong, with a dash of milk and no sugar, please.' And then Jane did a double take as she saw the pram in the corner of the living room. 'Have you two been shopping or something?'

'No—it's a loan from the sister of one of my colleagues,' he said. 'She lent us a snowsuit as well, so we took Hope for a walk in the park across the road today. I think she enjoyed her first trip out.'

'And her temperature's normal again?' Jane asked.

'Yes. We wouldn't have taken her out if we'd been in the slightest bit worried about her—that's why we left it until today,' Amy said. 'She's doing fine. We weighed her this morning and she's put on two ounces.'

'You've borrowed baby scales?' Jane asked.

'Not exactly.' Josh and Amy shared a glance and grinned.

'What am I missing?' Jane asked.

'We improvised,' Josh said. 'It involved Amy's kitchen scales, a towel and a baking tray.'

Jane laughed. 'Well, clearly it worked. And you both look very comfortable with her.'

'We've had our moments,' Josh said wryly. 'She really hates having baths. You have to sing her through them.'

'But I can show you her sleep and feed charts,' Amy said. 'And we're doing a book of her first days, either for her mum or for Hope herself. We're including photos and what have you, so Hope—and her mum—don't feel they've missed anything in the future.'

'That's really sweet of you,' Jane said, accepting the mug of tea gratefully from Josh.

'Do you have any news for us?' Josh asked.

'About Freya?' She grimaced. 'I'm telling you this unofficially, because strictly speaking this should all be confidential, but I need some help—and, because it's your theory, I think you're the best ones to give me advice.'

'Why do you need help?' Amy asked, confused.

'I went to the house, but Freya's mum refused to let me in,' Jane said. 'She was quite difficult with me, so my gut feeling tells me that she has something to hide. If Freya definitely hadn't had a baby, all she had to do was call the girl down and let me see her, and I could've ticked whatever box on a form and gone away again.'

'Unless she didn't actually know that Freya had had the baby. Amy, you said she was wearing baggy clothes at school?' Josh asked.

Amy nodded.

'So she might have done the same at home. Freya could have hidden the pregnancy from her mum, had the baby—well, wherever—then gone straight home again after she'd left the baby on our doorstep. If she told her mum that she was having a really bad period, that would explain why she was bleeding so much after the birth. She's at the age where periods are still all over the place, and some girls get quite severe period pains,' Josh said thoughtfully.

'And Freya's mum did say that there were problems with the stepfather. Maybe there had been a huge row or something,' Amy suggested, 'and one of the neighbours had tried to intervene, and Freya's mum thought that someone had called you to complain about the way she was treating her daughter.'

'I still think she's hiding something. She wouldn't look me in the eye,' Jane said. 'Does Freya have a close friend she might have confided in?'

'Her best friend Alice is the most likely person,' Amy said.

'Do you have her details? And this comes under the safeguarding stuff for Freya, if you're worrying about data protection,' Jane added quickly.

Amy powered up her laptop, logged into the school system and wrote Alice's details down for Jane.

'I could have an unofficial word with her, maybe,' Amy suggested.

Jane shook her head. 'No, you need to leave this to official channels. If Alice tells me something helpful then I can do something to help Freya.' She sighed. 'Poor kid. I kind of hope your theory's wrong.'

'So do I,' Josh said, 'but I have a nasty feeling that we're right.'

'I'll be in touch, then,' Jane said. 'And thank you for everything you're doing. Obviously we'll get you financial recompense for—'

'No,' Amy cut in. 'It's nice to be able to do something practical to help. Call it a Christmas gift to Hope and her mum.'

'Seconded,' Josh said firmly. 'We're not doing this for the money.'

'OK. Well, thank you,' Jane said. 'I'll go and have a word with Alice.'

When the social worker had gone, Josh looked at Amy. 'Are you all right?'

She nodded. 'Just thinking about Freya.'

'Hopefully Jane can intervene and get her the help she needs,' Josh said. 'Hey. I could cook us dinner tonight.'

'Seriously?'

'Seriously. You've made me rethink about my cooking skills, since you taught me how to make that salmon thing.'

'OK. That'd be lovely.'

'I'll just go and get some supplies,' he said. 'I can't keep raiding your fridge.'

'You mean, I don't have anything in my kitchen that you can actually cook,' she teased.

He grinned. 'Busted.'

'I'll print out the photos we've taken of Hope and stick them in her book while you're gone,' she said.

'And label them,' he said, 'because your handwriting's a lot neater than mine.'

'Agreed.'

'Anything you need from the shops?'

'No, it's fine.' She kissed him lingeringly. 'See you later.'

In the supermarket, Josh bought ingredients for spaghetti Bolognese. Pudding would definitely have to be shop-bought, he thought, and was delighted to discover a tiramisu cheesecake in the chiller cabinet. He knew Amy liked coffee ice cream, so this looked like a safe bet.

And then he walked through the healthcare aisle and saw the condoms.

He didn't have any, and he guessed that she didn't either. It wasn't quite making an assumption; tonight wasn't going to be the night. But at some point in the future he was pretty sure that they were going to make love, and it would be sensible for them to have protection available. And he had a feeling Amy would be a lot more comfortable using condoms than any other kind of contraception, given her history.

Putting the packet of condoms in his basket felt weird. He hadn't even had to think about this for a long time; during most of their relationship, Kelly had been on the Pill. Or so he'd thought. He couldn't even remember the last time he'd bought condoms. But this made him feel like a teenager, nervous and excited all at the same time.

He shook himself and added a bottle of Pinot Grigio to his basket. And then, by the checkouts, he saw the stand of flowers. He couldn't resist buying a bunch for Amy—nothing flashy and over-the-top that would make her feel awkward and embarrassed, but some pretty gerberas and roses in shades of dark red and pink.

When he got back to the flat, she greeted him with a kiss.

'For you,' he said, handing her the flowers with a flourish.

She looked delighted. 'They're gorgeous. Thank you. That's so sweet—you didn't have to.'

'Apart from the fact that men are supposed to buy their girlfriends flowers, and you're officially my girlfriend,' he pointed out, 'I wanted to.'

She hugged him. 'And I love them. Gerberas are my favourite flowers.'

'More luck than judgement,' he said. 'And I've cheated on the pudding.'

'Need me to do anything to help after I've put these in water?'

'Nope. Though I'd better run the pudding by you, in case you hate it.'

'Oh, nice choice, Dr Farnham,' she said when he showed her the box. 'Tiramisu and cheesecake—there isn't a more perfect combination.'

He laughed. 'Just don't look at the nutritional label, OK?'

'Would that be doctor's orders?' she teased.

'It would.' He smiled at her. 'Go and sit down and carry on with whatever you were doing.'

'Reading a gory crime novel.'

'Go and sit down and I'll make dinner.'

She looked intrigued. 'So is it going to be a cheese toastie or the famous spaghetti Bolognese?'

'Wait and see.'

Except it went disastrously wrong. Not only did he burn the sauce badly enough to ruin the meal, he actually set off the smoke alarm.

And Hope took great exception to the smoke alarm. She even managed to drown it out with her screams.

Amy walked into the kitchen, jiggling the screaming baby in an attempt to calm her. 'Open the windows and flap a damp tea-towel underneath the smoke alarm,' she said. 'I set it off when I first moved in and my toaster decided not to pop the toast out again after it was done.'

It didn't make him feel any better, but he followed her instructions and eventually the smoke alarm stopped shrieking.

Hope, on the other hand, took a fair bit longer to

stop shrieking, and he'd completely run out of songs by the time Amy had warmed some milk and given the baby an unscheduled feed in an attempt to stop her screaming.

'Sorry. I don't *think* I've ruined your saucepan. But it's a close-run thing.' He grimaced. 'And there's no way I can serve up dinner.'

But Amy didn't seem fazed in the slightest. She just laughed. 'These things happen. Stick the saucepan in water and we'll soak it for a while. I'm sure it will have survived. And we'll get a takeaway for dinner. Do you fancy Indian, Chinese or pizza?'

'Pizza. And I'm buying, because dinner was supposed to be my treat tonight,' he said ruefully.

'We'll go halves,' she said, 'and you do the washing up.'

'Including the burned saucepan. Deal.' He sighed. 'It's the last time I try to impress you,' he grumbled.

She kissed him. 'Don't try to impress me. Just be yourself.'

Being himself instead of being who other people wanted him to be was what had led to a rift between himself and his family, and he was pretty sure it had also contributed a fair bit to the breakdown of his marriage.

But then again, Amy wasn't anything like Kelly or his family. Maybe it would be different with her. Maybe he'd be enough for her.

He hoped.

After the pizza—and after, to Josh's relief, he'd managed to get her saucepan perfectly clean—they spent another evening of what really felt like domestic bliss. Amy switched on her stereo and played music by some gentle singer-songwriters that had Hope snoozing comfortably, while the two of them played cards for a while and then stretched out on the sofa together, spooned together with his arms wrapped round her waist and his cheek against hers.

He couldn't remember feeling this chilled-out and happy for a long, long time. They didn't even need to talk: it was enough just to be together, relaxing and enjoying each other's warmth.

Later that evening, when Hope had had her last feed of the evening and they'd gone to bed, he found their goodnight kisses turning hotter, to the point where they were both uncovering bare skin.

He stopped. 'I don't want to rush you.'

Her skin heated. 'Sorry. You're right. We shouldn't take this too fast.'

Though he wanted to. And the expression in her gorgeous brown eyes told him that she might want to, too. He stroked her face. 'I, um, bought stuff today in the supermarket. Just in case. Not because I expect it, but… Well. Later. When we're both ready.'

She kissed him. 'We have kind of known each other for months.'

'Just not very well,' he added in fairness.

Was it his imagination, or had her pupils just gone wider?

'Maybe it's time we remedied that.'

He went very still. 'Are you sure?'

She kissed him. 'Very sure. Because the way you make me feel… I haven't felt that in a long, long time.'

'Same here,' he said.

'Then maybe we ought to seize the day.'

'Carpe diem,' he agreed.

He fetched the condoms, and checked that the baby was OK. And then there was nothing left to hold them back.

CHAPTER EIGHT

Wednesday

'So ARE YOU back on duty today?' Amy asked.

'I'm afraid so,' Josh said. 'But I'm on a late shift, so I thought maybe we could take Hope out for a walk this morning and make the most of the sunshine.'

'Sounds good to me,' she said, smiling.

How much things had changed since Christmas Eve. Just five short days: and in that time Amy had grown much more confident with the baby.

She'd grown much more confident in herself, too. For the last eighteen months, she'd felt as if she wasn't good enough to be anyone's partner, because she couldn't offer them a family and a future. Josh had shown her just how mistaken she was. And last night, when they'd made love, he'd been so gentle with her, so tender.

Even catching his eye right now made her feel hot all over, remembering how his hands had felt against her skin, how his mouth had coaxed a response she hadn't even known she was capable of.

And Josh seemed different, too. Even though he'd told her everything about his past, she'd sensed a kind of barrier still there: as if he didn't trust anyone enough to let them see who he really was. After last night, that barrier was gone.

Walking along the riverside, hand in hand with Josh and pushing the pram, made Amy feel as if the world was full of sunshine.

And then her mobile phone rang.

'Amy Howes,' she said.

'Amy, it's Jane Richards. Where are you?'

'With Hope and Josh, by the river.' Amy went cold. The deal was that they'd be looking after Hope until New Year's Eve. There could only be two reasons why Jane was calling: either she'd found Hope's mother, or she'd found a permanent foster carer. 'Is something wrong?' she asked, knowing that the answer would be 'yes'—at least from her perspective.

'I need to see you, I'm afraid. Can I meet you at your flat?'

She took a deep breath. 'OK. We can be back in fifteen minutes.'

'Great. I'll be there,' Jane said.

Amy hung up and turned to Josh. 'You've probably already worked out that that was Jane.'

'She's found Hope's mum?'

'She didn't say. But it's either that or she's found a more permanent set of foster parents.' She held her breath for a moment in the hope that it would stop her bursting into tears.

This was ridiculous.

She'd always known that this was a temporary situation. That they'd be looking after Hope until New Year's Eve at the latest, and then they'd have to give her back.

But she'd already bonded with the baby. She'd learned the difference between a cry to say Hope was hungry, a cry to say she needed a fresh nappy, and a cry to say she wanted a cuddle. Josh, too.

Without the baby bonding them together, was this thing between them too new and too fragile to survive? Would she lose Josh as well as the baby?

'Hey. We always knew we'd have to give her back,' Josh said softly.

'I know. But I'll…' To her horror, Amy felt a tear sliding down her face.

Josh drew her into his arms and held her close. 'Miss her,' he finished. 'Me, too. It's going to be strange without Munchkin around.'

And they'd go back to living in their separate flats. Next week, term would start again and Josh would be working very different hours from hers. Would they manage to keep seeing each other? Josh himself had said how difficult it was to find time to date someone when you worked shifts.

'Amy. I take it she wants to see us?'

Amy nodded.

'When?'

'Now.' It felt as if she was forcing the word past a massive lump in her throat.

His arms tightened round her. 'Then we need to go back.'

To face the beginning of the end?

'I know,' she said softly, and made the effort to pull herself together.

Jane was waiting in the lobby by the time they got back to their block.

'I'll make tea,' Josh said. 'Strong, a dash of milk, no sugar, right?'

'Thank you,' Jane said.

Back in her flat, Amy took Hope out of the pram and her snowsuit. So this was the last time she was going to hold her. The baby Amy had promised herself she wouldn't bond with—and yet she had. This was the last cuddle. The last time she'd smell that soft powdery baby scent. The last time she'd see those beautiful dark blue eyes.

She couldn't say a word. All she could do was cuddle the baby and wish that things were different.

Jane waited until Josh was back with them and sitting next to Amy before she told them what had happened.

'This is in strictest confidence,' the social worker warned. 'I shouldn't even be telling you any of this— but without you we wouldn't have found out the full story, so I think you have a right to know. Just...' She grimaced.

'We know. And we'll keep it to ourselves,' Josh said.

'I went to see Alice, first thing this morning.' Jane bit her lip. 'She told me everything.'

'So were we right and Freya is Hope's mother?' Amy asked.

'Yes. But she doesn't have a boyfriend.' Jane took a deep breath. 'It's pretty nasty. You know you said she wasn't getting on with her mum's new partner?'

'Oh, no.' Amy felt her eyes widen as she guessed at the horrible truth. 'Please tell me he didn't interfere with her.'

Jane grimaced. 'Unfortunately, he did a lot more

than that. Freya told her mum what was happening, but she wouldn't believe the girl.'

'Surely she must've known what was going on?' Josh asked.

'Not necessarily,' Amy said. 'When I talked to her, she said that Freya was jealous and being difficult. Maybe she thought that Freya was lying about the guy to break them up and get her mother's full attention back—or even make the space to get her father back with her mother again.'

'It's easy to judge when you're outside the situation,' Jane agreed. 'She might not have known what was happening—or she might have refused to see it because she didn't want to face the truth.'

'So then Freya became pregnant?' Josh asked.

Jane nodded. 'She said she didn't know what to do when she found out.'

'I wish she'd come to me,' Amy said.

'That's what Alice's mum said, too. Between the two of you, I think you would've helped the poor child,' Jane said. 'Freya said she thought about talking to you, but she was scared you wouldn't believe her, either.'

'Poor girl. I would've listened. Why didn't Alice come and see me? She's in my form, too.'

'Freya swore Alice to secrecy,' Jane said. 'Alice agreed, but only on condition Freya promised to have the baby in hospital. She told me she thought that if Freya had the baby in hospital, someone there would get her to tell the truth and they'd help her.'

'But obviously she didn't go to hospital when she started having contractions. There's no way they would have discharged her from the ward, even with the virus situation at the hospital,' Josh said. 'Plus the baby had one of those freezer clips as a cord clamp. It looked to me as if the mum had read up about birth and was doing the best she possibly could.'

'The baby was a couple of weeks early. I guess it took her by surprise,' Jane said. 'She had the baby in the shed at home.'

Amy winced. 'In the middle of winter, all on her own, with no support. That poor child. Has she gone to hospital now?'

Jane nodded. 'I took her there myself. She's being checked over properly.'

'What about the stepfather?' Josh asked.

'I spoke to the police on the way to Freya's. They have him in custody.'

'I sincerely hope they throw the book at him and make sure he can never, ever do that to another girl,' Amy said.

'They will,' Jane reassured her.

Amy knew she had to be brave and ask the question. 'So what happens to Hope?'

'She's going to stay with Freya for a day or two, until Freya decides what she wants to do—whether she wants to keep the baby or give her up for adoption,' Jane said. 'I've got an infant seat in the car, so I can take her with me now.'

'Where are they going to stay?' Josh asked.

'Probably at the hospital—though I know there are the virus problems still, so maybe they'll go back to her mother's,' Jane said.

Amy frowned. 'Is that really a good idea? Especially if the stepfather gets out on bail?'

'Or we'll find her a safe place,' Jane said. 'It depends on what Freya wants to do.'

'I'm glad you're taking what she wants into account,' Josh said. 'It sounds to me as if the poor girl hasn't really had anyone on her side for a long time.' He looked at Amy. 'Though obviously you would've been there for her, if she'd given you the chance.'

'Yeah.' And now Freya wanted her baby back. 'I guess I'd better get Hope's stuff together,' Amy said. Keeping busy was the best way to get through this. She handed the baby to Josh, then went to bag up the sleep suits that Jane had brought, the Moses basket and bedding and bottles and sterilising equipment.

Funny, all that extra stuff should've made her flat feel cluttered. It hadn't. And, without the baby, the place was going to feel so empty.

Stupid of her to fall in love with the baby.

And equally stupid of her to fall in love with Josh.

Because there wasn't going to be a happy ending. Didn't they say be careful what you wish for? What they didn't say was that you might get what you really wanted but then have to give it back.

'I need to wash the stuff that Alison's sister lent us,' she said. 'And we've got the necklace that Freya left with Hope—she needs that. And the book we did, with her sleep chart and feed chart and weight, and pictures of her first few days and—' Her voice caught.

'I'm sorry,' Jane said. 'You've both been brilliant.'

'We're just going to miss her, that's all,' Josh said. 'We've got used to her being around.'

'Of course you have.'

Josh kissed the baby's forehead. 'Well, Munchkin, look after yourself.'

The baby grizzled, as if picking up on the dark mood in the room.

'Goodbye, Hope,' Amy whispered, unable to bear holding the baby again because she knew just how hard it would be to hand her over to the social worker.

'I'll be in touch,' Jane said.

'I'll walk you down to your car. Carry the stuff,' Josh offered.

'And I'd better start washing the things that Alison lent us,' Amy said. She didn't think she could handle watching Jane drive away with the baby.

She half expected Josh not to come back, but he knocked on her door when he'd seen Jane into her car.

'Are you OK?' he asked.

What was the point in lying? 'Not really.'

'I'll ring work and see if I can swap shifts with someone,' he said.

'No. They need you at the hospital,' Amy said.

Meaning that you don't? Josh wondered, but didn't dare to ask. Just in case that was what she said. Right now, he could see that she was hurting. He knew that when people were hurt they often said things they didn't mean but the words still caused an awful lot of damage. It would be better to back off now and regroup.

He glanced at his watch. 'Actually, I do have to go, if you're sure you don't want me to try and change my shift.'

When she said nothing, he sighed inwardly. 'I'll be home as soon as I can,' he promised.

Amy turned away. 'Sorry. I think I just need some time on my own.'

Did that mean she didn't want him to come over after work?

As if he'd spoken out loud, she said, 'I'll see you tomorrow, maybe.'

Josh went cold.

He hadn't been enough for Kelly.

And, now the baby wasn't here, Amy didn't need his help any more. She didn't need him. So he wasn't enough for her, either. What kind of delusional fool was he, to think this was going to work out?

'OK. Call me if you need me,' he said, but he knew she wouldn't.

And it was pointless trying to put his arms round her and kiss her, or tell her that everything was going to be all right. He'd seen that closed-off look with Kelly, too, and he knew what it meant.

The end.

So it was over almost as soon as it had started, Amy thought as Josh closed her front door behind him.

This morning, she'd been so happy. She'd had everything she ever wanted. A baby, and a partner who cared about her—a partner who was a decent man, one who wouldn't lie or cheat or let her down.

Except, now the baby had gone, Josh had walked away from her just as easily as Michael had. No doubt he'd been relieved when she'd said she wanted some time on her own. It meant he hadn't had to do the 'it's not you, it's me' speech.

Well, she'd pick herself up, dust herself down, and remember not to let people too close again in future.

Josh was too busy at work to get a chance to pop up to the maternity ward to see if Freya and Hope were there. When he'd finished his shift, it was too late to visit; if Freya was still on the ward, he thought, the poor girl would probably be asleep.

He walked home, and paused outside Amy's door. Should he knock and see how she was doing?

Then again, she'd said she wanted space. And she hadn't texted him, even though she knew he'd pick up any messages as soon as he'd finished his shift.

Well, he wasn't going to give up on her that easily. He knocked on the door. 'Amy? Are you there?'

She didn't answer.

He tried her mobile. A recorded voice informed him that the phone was switched off and he should leave a message or send a text.

Right.

He was pretty sure she wouldn't reply to those, either.

With a heavy heart, he carried on down the corridor to his own flat. Funny how empty the place seemed. And was it his imagination or did the place smell musty?

At least cleaning everything kept him too busy to think for a little while. He didn't bother making himself a sandwich because he just wasn't hungry. But when it came to bedtime... His double bed felt way too wide. It was worse than when he'd first moved in to the flat, because now he knew what it would feel like if the place was really home rather than simply a place to sleep and store his clothes.

But he wasn't enough for Amy, just as he hadn't been enough for Kelly. He'd just have to get used to that. And he was never going to risk his heart again.

CHAPTER NINE

Thursday

JOSH ACTUALLY TOOK his break at lunchtime, the next day, and paid a quiet visit to the maternity ward rather than heading for the canteen.

'Hey, Josh—are you coming up to see us, for a change? Usually you call us down to the Emergency Department to see a patient,' one of the obstetricians teased.

'Actually, I haven't come to see you—I've come to visit a friend of a friend during my lunch break,' he said. And that was sort of true. If you could count a week-old baby as a friend.

'Who?'

'Freya. If she's still here. I know she and the baby came in yesterday.'

His colleague frowned. 'Oh, our young missing mum? Yes, she's here. She's—' He stopped.

'Patient confidentiality,' Josh said with a sigh. 'I know. Does it help if you know I looked after the baby?'

'Downstairs?'

'Yes.' It wasn't a total stretch of the truth—he and

Amy *had* brought Hope in to the Emergency Department, and he had indeed been looking after Hope... Albeit as a stand-in parent, rather than as a doctor.

'Ah. Well, if we're talking as fellow clinicians, the baby's doing fine. Freya does have an infection, but we've put her on antibiotics and it should clear up in a couple of days. We're keeping her in for the moment to keep an eye on her.'

'Great.' Josh gave his sweetest smile. 'Can I put my head round the door for two seconds and say hello?'

'Actually, it might do the poor kid good to have a visitor,' the obstetrician said. 'Sure.'

'Thanks. Where do I find her?'

'She's in room six.'

Even better: Freya was in a room on her own, so she wouldn't be embarrassed about their conversation being overheard. 'Great. Thanks.'

He knocked on the door of room six, then went in when he heard Freya call, 'Yes?'

'Hello,' he said with a smile. 'Freya, isn't it?'

She looked at him, her eyes wide and suddenly full of fear. 'Have you come to take the baby? Are you from the police?'

'No and no,' he reassured her. The poor kid was really upset, and she could do with a bit of handholding, he thought. He knew the perfect person to do that, but right now he had a feeling that Amy's head might not be in the right place. 'And you're not in trouble. My name's Josh and I'm a doctor,' he said, indicating his white coat and his hospital identity card.

'I haven't seen you before. Are you from the maternity ward?' she asked.

'No, I'm from the Emergency Department.'

She frowned. 'But I haven't been in an accident or anything. Why do you need to see me?'

'Actually,' he said, 'I came to say hello to you and to see how Munchkin's doing.'

'Munchkin?' Freya looked confused.

'Hope,' he explained.

She frowned again. 'Why do you call her Munchkin?'

'Because she's tiny—you know, like the people in *The Wizard of Oz*.'

'Oh. And how do you know her name's Hope?'

He could understand why the poor girl was so suspicious. She'd been through a lot. Right then, he really wanted to give her a hug and tell her everything was going to work out just fine, but it wouldn't be appropriate. Plus, given what had happened to her, the contact from a strange man would probably worry her even more. 'Because,' he said quietly, 'I'm Miss Howes's neighbour and I've been helping her look after the baby for the last week.'

'Oh.' Freya bit her lip. 'Sorry. I ruined your Christmas.'

'On the contrary,' he said. 'I was planning to have a really lousy Christmas on my own, doing my shift downstairs and then eating my body weight in left-over sausage rolls that hadn't been stored properly and probably ending up with food poisoning—and because of you I had a decent Christmas dinner cooked for me and I got to spend Christmas with someone really nice.'

There was the hint of a smile, just for a moment, and then her expression switched back to gloom again.

'So can I give her a cuddle?' he asked.

'I guess.'

He picked the baby up, and settled down with her on the chair next to Freya's bed. 'Hey, Munchkin. I know you're asleep so you're not going to answer, but have you missed Uncle Joshy's terrible singing?'

Freya blinked in surprise. 'You sing to her?'

'Yup. Little tip from me—you'll need to do that a lot when she has a bath,' he said. 'She absolutely hates baths. She screams the place down.'

'What do you sing to her?'

'Anything. She doesn't care what it is, as long as you sing,' he said with a smile. And he was relieved that finally Freya seemed to be responding to him. 'So how are *you* doing?' he asked, trying to keep his voice as gentle and non-threatening as possible.

She shrugged. 'OK, I suppose.'

Well, it was probably a stupid question. He went back to safer ground. 'Hope's a really beautiful baby, you know. And her name fits her perfectly.'

A tear slid down her cheek. 'And I'm going to have to give her away.'

'Why?'

'I'm fifteen. I'm supposed to be at school.' She shook her head, looking anguished. 'I can't go to school with a baby, can I?'

'Won't your mum help?'

'No chance.' Freya gave a snort of disgust. 'She hates me—and I hate her, too.'

'Hate's a very strong word,' he said softly. 'Families can be complicated, and sometimes they can make you feel as if you've let them down. And sometimes you feel that they're the ones who let you down.'

'She thinks it's all my fault. The baby.'

He waited, giving Freya the space to find the words.

'She thinks I led him on. But I didn't.'

'I know,' he said gently.

She looked shocked. 'You believe me?'

'Yes.'

'*She* doesn't.'

'Maybe your mum just needs a bit of time to think about it,' he suggested.

'She won't change her mind.' Freya dragged in a breath. 'And I know she wants him back.'

He could understand exactly why Freya didn't want to live with her stepfather again. He didn't want the girl having to live with the man again, either. He'd quite like to rearrange the man's body parts, except he knew that violence didn't solve anything and locking the man away for a long time was a better option. 'Maybe there's another way,' he said. 'Jane, the social worker, is really nice. She might be able to find you a foster family who'll look after you and the baby.'

Freya's expression was filled with disbelief. 'Who's going to take on a fifteen-year-old and a baby? I'm going to end up in a children's home, and everyone's going to despise me.'

'There are nice people out there. People who are kind. People who help others.' He paused. 'That's why you rang Miss Howes's doorbell, isn't it?'

Freya nodded. 'She's my form teacher. Everyone loves her, because she's kind and funny.'

Yeah. And Amy had been his, for just a little while. Being without her made his heart ache.

'I knew she'd look after the baby and know what to do,' Freya continued.

'Maybe you could've talked to her when you found out you were pregnant,' he said.

'I wanted to—Alice, she's my best friend, she said I ought to, but I made her promise she wouldn't tell anyone, not even her mum.' Freya bit her lip. 'I would've told Miss Howes about *him*, but I was scared. He said if I told anyone he'd make sure nobody believed me and I'd get taken into care.'

Being taken into care probably would've been the best thing for her, Josh thought. It would have got her away from the man who'd been systematically abusing her. 'Miss Howes would've believed you. Luckily Alice did tell her mum in the end,' he said, 'because you needed antibiotics and you could've been very ill without them.' He paused. 'Would Alice's mum let you stay with them, maybe?'

Freya shook her head. 'They don't have enough room. There isn't a spare bedroom, and Alice's bedroom is too small for more than one bed, let alone another bed and a cot. So I don't know what's going to happen to me.'

'There are nice people in the world, Freya,' he said again, 'and Jane will make sure someone really nice looks after you and Hope, if you want to keep her.'

'I do.' Freya glanced down at the baby. 'Even though she's his—well, she's a girl, so she won't look like him and she won't remind me of him.'

'She's gorgeous. She's definitely got your nose and chin,' he said.

'Thank you,' she said, 'for looking after Hope for me.'

'It was a pleasure,' he said, meaning it. 'We did a notebook for her first few days—we wrote down when she slept and when she had some milk, and took some photographs.'

'I know—Miss Richards gave it to me. Thank you.'

'You've probably already worked it out for yourself, but mine's the terrible handwriting,' he said.

'Who did the drawings in the back?' she asked.

'Me,' he said.

'You're good.'

He inclined his head in acknowledgement. 'Thank you.'

'Why aren't you an artist instead of a doctor?' she asked.

'It's how things worked out,' he said. 'Sometimes, your plans don't work out quite as you thought they would, but you can still find a chance to be happy.'

'I guess,' she said, sounding unconvinced, but he hoped that she'd think about what he'd said and realise that he was telling the truth. 'Would you tell Miss Howes thanks for me?'

'Sure,' he said. Though he might have to do it by text, if she was avoiding him.

'And sorry. She's really kind. I know I shouldn't have just dumped Hope in that blanket in a cardboard box, but I just didn't know what to do.'

'Hey.' He patted her hand. 'You were having a tough time. And you knew Amy—Miss Howes—would make sure Hope was all right, so that was one thing less you had to worry about.'

'Yeah.' She sniffed.

'I've got to go back to work, now,' he said. 'But maybe I can come and see you and Hope again tomorrow?'

'I'd like that,' she said.

'And I'll bring my sketchbook. Do you a proper picture of you both together.' He stroked the baby's face. 'Nice to see you, Munchkin. Even if you weren't going to wake up and say hello.' Gently, he transferred the baby back to Freya's arms. 'If you need anything, get them to call me. Josh Farnham in Emergency. They know me up here anyway,' he said.

Freya's eyes filled with tears. 'That's so kind. Thank you.'

And not enough people had been kind to the girl, he thought savagely. He'd quite like a little chat with Freya's mother about how to treat a child properly—and she'd be squirming so much by the time he'd finished, she'd treat the girl decently for ever after. 'No worries, Freya,' he said. 'Take care.'

He thought about it through the rest of the day. Freya's assessment of Amy: *Everyone loves her, because she's kind and funny.*

Amy was more than that. Much more.

She made him feel as if the sun had come out after a week of pouring rain.

And the week they'd just shared... Yes, it had been intense, almost like being snowbound but without the snow: but it hadn't just been the baby holding them together. What they had was real.

She'd definitely pushed him away, yesterday. And, now he thought about it, he realised why. She was kind and funny and nice—and she was trying to do what she thought was best for him. Setting him free to find someone who could give him the family he wanted without any complications.

Except if she'd actually said that to him, he would've had the chance to tell her that it wasn't what he wanted. Yes, he wanted a family; but he wanted her more. He needed to convince her that it didn't matter if they couldn't have children. And maybe he needed to prove to her that he could be enough for her, the way he hadn't been enough for Kelly. What they had was too good to throw away.

He actually ran home, after his shift.

And this time he didn't knock on Amy's door; instead, he rang her buzzer on the intercom.

When she didn't answer, he wondered for a moment if she'd gone out. But something told him she was home alone, feeling as miserable as he did without her. There was only one way he could think of to make her talk to him: to lean on the buzzer, and not stop until she answered.

'Yes?' She sounded cross and miserable at the same time.

'Amy, it's Josh. We need to talk.'

'I—'

'No excuses and no refusals,' he said. 'We really do need to talk, Amy. Just give me five minutes. Please.'

She sighed. 'You didn't have to lean on the buzzer. You could've just knocked on my door.'

'And you would've ignored me, like you did last night,' he pointed out. 'Can I come in?'

She sighed again. 'I don't have any choice, do I?'

'Nope,' he said. 'We need to talk.' If she said no after she'd listened to what he had to say, then fair enough—he'd accept that. But he needed to tell her how he felt, and she needed to know what was going on in his head. The only way that was going to happen was if they talked instead of avoiding the issues.

'See you in a second,' she said.

It took him more like twenty seconds to get to her door, but at least this time she opened it when he knocked.

And she looked as if she hadn't slept. There were dark hollows under her eyes and her face was lined with misery.

'How are you doing?' he asked.

'Not brilliant,' she admitted.

Even though he'd meant to keep at arm's length until they'd talked, he couldn't just stand there and let her feel awful. He wrapped his arms round her and held her close. 'I know. Me, too. And I've missed you even more than I miss Hope.'

'Josh, I—'

'Please, just let me talk,' he said. 'If you say no when you've heard me out, I won't push you. But don't say no before you've heard what I have to say.'

'OK.' She wriggled out of his arms. 'Let's sit down. Coffee?'

'No, thanks.' He knew it was a delaying tactic, and he didn't want to wait any more. He wanted to get this sorted out right now. He followed her in to the living room and sat next to her on the sofa. 'I went to see Freya and Hope today.'

Her eyes widened. 'How are they?'

'Doing OK,' he said. 'Freya wants to keep the baby, but she doesn't want to go back to live with her mum—and she's worried about how school's going to work, with a baby.'

'We can support her,' Amy said. 'We can do a lot to help, now we know about the situation.'

He smiled. 'I knew you'd say that. And she also said she rang your doorbell because she knew you'd look after the baby and you'd know what to do.' He paused. 'She says everyone loves you, because you're kind and funny.'

Amy blinked, and he had the strongest impression that she was close to tears. 'That's nice.'

'You're more than that,' he said. 'And that's why I want to talk to you.' This time, he reached over to take her hand. 'I know this is fast and I know we both have issues from the past we'll still have to work through. But I like you—no, I more than like you, Amy.' He might as well tell her the whole lot. 'Over the last week, I've fallen in love with you. Not because of the baby, but because you're bright and you're funny and you're warm, and you have this whole aura about you that makes me feel as if the sun's just come out after a week of rain. And I know that sounds flowery and cheesy and maybe even a bit smarmy, but it's not meant to be like that.' He threw his free hand up into the air in exasperation. 'I just don't have any better words to describe it.'

'Oh, Josh.'

The expression on her face gave him hope, so he pushed on.

'I know Michael left you because you couldn't have children, but he was an idiot. He was missing the point. And I'm not Michael. Yes, I always thought I wanted a family, and spending this last week looking after Hope with you made me realise that I do still want that. But it doesn't matter that you can't have children. We did a great job as foster parents for Hope, this week, and we could do that again for another child.'

'But it's still a massive compromise,' Amy said. 'I wasn't enough for Michael.'

'And I wasn't enough for Kelly. But you're not Kelly, and I'm not Michael.' He paused. 'You're enough for me. You're everything I want. And I want you with or without a family, Amy.'

'I'm not brilliant at relationships. Not long-term,' she said. 'There was Gavin.'

'Who cheated on you. He was a snake.'

'And Michael.'

'Who was a selfish toad. I don't think your problem's with relationships, Amy—it's that you pick amphibians.'

She winced. 'Don't pull your punches.'

'There's no point in trying to sugar-coat things. You and me, we're about honesty. So we know we can trust each other. I've got my faults, just like everyone else, but I'm most definitely not a reptile,' he said. 'So do something different, this time, to make it work. Pick a man who's not a snake or a toad. Pick me.'

Could she really believe this?

Would she be enough for Josh?

Then again, she knew he had a similar issue, feeling that he hadn't been enough for his ex-wife. They were coming from the same sort of place and wanted the same sort of things.

'Pick me, Amy,' he said again, his voice soft. 'Because I choose you, too.'

'We haven't even gone out on a date together,' she said.

'Yeah—our relationship has been a bit backwards, so far. Baby first, then...' He smiled. 'Well.'

Sex. Amy's skin heated at the memories.

'Let's go out on a date tonight,' he said. 'I need a shower, but whatever I do to my hair it's going to look like this within five minutes, so I hope you'll forgive the fact that it looks a mess.'

'There's nothing wrong with your hair. It's cute.' And then, just because he looked a little bit worried and she thought he needed a bit of reassurance, she ran her fingers through his hair to smooth it slightly. 'Sexy,' she said.

'You think I'm sexy?'

'I think you're a lot of things.' And because he'd said it all first, she had the courage to say it back to him. 'You're kind and you're caring and you're reliable. You're calm in a crisis. And it scares the hell out of me that we've been on nod-and-smile terms for six months, but we've just spent a week together like a real family, and somewhere along the way I fell in love with you and I never expected anything like that to happen.'

'And you're still scared it's going to go wrong,' he said.

She nodded.

'Me, too. But we can work on that,' he said. 'Together. How long's it going to take you to get ready?'

'How dressy are we talking?'

'I know a bistro not too far from here where they do live music,' he said. 'And I patched up the chef six months ago, so I'm pretty sure they'll be able to find us a table for two.'

'Little black dress and lipstick, and do something with my hair—that'll be about twenty minutes,' she calculated swiftly.

'Deal.' He looked at her. 'And we're supposed to seal a deal, aren't we?'

In answer, she leaned forward and kissed him.

And he kissed her back until her knees went weak.

'Twenty minutes,' he said, and headed for the door. Then he leaned back round the doorframe. 'I love you,' he said, blew her another kiss, and left.

Yesterday, when Amy had had to give Hope back—even though she'd known it was going to happen—had been one of the hardest days of her life. A real emotional roller coaster that had left her miserable and lonely and aching.

Today, it felt as if she'd climbed all the way back to the top. Except this time there wasn't a sharp descent back into the shadows.

A bistro with live music. Dressy but not *too* dressy, then.

The little black dress, tights and lipstick took a couple of minutes. Her hair took slightly longer, pulled into a loose up-do with a few strands left to frame her face and soften the effect.

And then Josh rang the doorbell.

How long was it since she'd gone on a proper date? Nerves throbbed through her, but she lifted her chin and strode over to answer the door.

In a dark suit with a white shirt buttoned to the neck but without a tie, and his hair sticking up all over the place, Josh looked sexy as hell. He took her breath away.

Clearly he was just as nervous as she was, because he opened his mouth to speak and nothing came out.

Crazy. They'd spent most of the last week together, talking about practically everything in the universe.

As if he was thinking exactly the same thing, he said, 'Um, this is insane. We talked all week. But now it's our first date and I don't know what to say to you.'

'Me, too,' she said. 'You look nice.'

'You look amazing,' he said. Then he grinned. 'But actually you still look amazing when your hair's all over the place and you've slept in your clothes, so I'm not being shallow.'

'Neither was I. But thank you for the compliment.' She inclined her head in acknowledgement.

'I feel like a teenager,' he said.

'Me, too.'

'But,' he said, 'I did definitely get us a table. So hopefully this won't be the date from hell.'

'Unless the heel of my shoe gets stuck in a grate and falls off, and I knock a glass of red wine across the table and ruin your shirt.'

'Or the chef does a body swap with me and I burn the spaghetti Bolognese again...'

She laughed and took his hand. 'I think we'll be all right.'

The restaurant turned out to have a wonderful menu, and the musician that night was a singer-song-writer who alternated between the guitar and the piano. And once the food and wine had relaxed them enough that they were at ease with each other again, it turned out to be the perfect date. They didn't stop talking through the meal, and then Josh held her hand as they enjoyed the music together.

They walked home along the riverside, their arms wrapped round each other, and Josh kissed Amy under every single lamp-post. Although it had turned cold, Amy didn't care; she was simply enjoying Josh's near-ness.

He paused outside her front door. 'I guess, as this is our first date, this is where I kiss you goodnight and wish you sweet dreams?'

'And I ask you in for coffee?' She spread her hands. 'Or there's the alternative version.'

His eyes darkened. 'Which is?'

'Sweet dreams, Josh.' She kissed him.

'And now I invite you in for coffee?' he asked.

She nodded.

Josh caught his breath as he realised exactly what she meant. 'And you stay?' he asked very softly.

'You've already seen my bedroom,' she said. 'And, if this is going to be an equal relationship...'

He didn't need a second invitation. He took her hand and led her to his flat.

He made coffee, as promised; but they didn't get to drink it because he ended up carrying her to his bed instead.

Afterwards, she fell asleep in his arms. This time neither of them wore pyjamas and there were no barriers between them. And Josh thought that maybe the future was going to work.

There was just one more thing that would make life perfect—and he'd suggest that to her in the morning.

CHAPTER TEN

Friday—New Year's Eve

THE NEXT MORNING, Josh woke, warm and comfortable.

Best of all, Amy was lying asleep in his arms.

And today was New Year's Eve. A time for new beginnings. A time, he hoped, for them to make a decision together that might just change everything for both of them.

He gently moved his arm from under her shoulder, and climbed out of bed without waking her. It took just a couple of minutes to throw on some clothes and brush his teeth, and he paused to write her a note just in case she woke while he was gone.

Gone to get breakfast.
Back in five minutes. x

He stuck the note to the inside of his front door, where she couldn't possibly miss it, and headed for the bakery just down the street.

When he returned, he peeked into his bedroom and Amy was just stirring.

'Well, good morning, sleepyhead,' he teased.

She squinted at him. 'Why are you dressed? Have you got to go to work?'

'Nope. I worked Christmas, so I get New Year's off,' he said. 'I'm dressed because I just went out to get us some breakfast.' He smiled. 'I did leave you a note on the front door in case you woke while I was away, but clearly you didn't. Stay where you are and I'll bring in the goodies.'

He came back two minutes later with a tray, a plate of warm croissants, jam and butter, and two mugs of coffee.

'You made coffee that fast?' she asked.

'No. I bought it from the bakery and I just poured it out of the paper cups into mugs,' he admitted. 'I didn't want to spend any more time away from you than I had to.'

'Croissants and proper coffee. The perfect breakfast in bed. Very decadent, Dr Farnham,' she said with a smile.

'I have a much better idea for being decadent, Miss Howes,' he said. 'How about Valentine's Day in Paris—proper Parisian croissants?'

'I really like the sound of that,' she said. 'But, if it's in term-time, I won't be able to take the day off. We might have to have an unofficial Valentine's Day instead.'

'Works for me,' he said.

Once they'd finished breakfast, he asked, 'What would you like to do today?'

'I really don't mind, as long as it's with you—or is that being greedy?'

'It's what I had in mind, too,' he said. 'Maybe we can go for a walk somewhere.'

'Sounds good to me,' she said, and kissed him. 'But I can hardly go out in last night's little black dress. I need to go next door and shower and change.'

'Thirty minutes?' he asked.

'That'd be great. Though I'll do the washing up first.'

'No. I'll do that while you get ready.' He kissed her again. 'Knock for me when you're done.'

Half an hour later, Amy knocked on Josh's door—having showered, washed her hair, dried it quickly and changed into jeans, a sweater and comfortable mid-heeled boots.

'You look beautiful,' he said, and kissed her.

'So do you.' She kissed him back. 'So where are we going?' she asked.

'I was thinking, maybe we can start by visiting Freya and Hope in hospital.'

'Are you sure they haven't been discharged?' she asked.

He nodded. 'I rang the ward and checked this morning.'

'Are we actually allowed to do this?'

He shrugged. 'Give me a good reason why you can't visit one of your pupils in hospital?'

'Because we've spent most of the past week looking after her baby?' Amy suggested.

'Then you're not visiting as her form tutor. You're visiting as a friend,' he pointed out.

'I'd like to see them,' Amy said. 'But we're not going empty-handed.'

'Good idea,' Josh said. 'They told me on the ward yesterday that she hadn't had any visitors.'

Amy looked shocked. 'Not even her mum, or her best friend?'

'Nope. That's why I said I'd pop in to see her today. And I promised I'd do a sketch of her and the baby together.' He indicated his sketchbook and pencils. 'Maybe I can get it framed for her.'

'That's a really lovely idea. And I agree, we should definitely make a fuss of her,' Amy said. 'Shops, first?'

'Absolutely.'

Between them, they found a couple of cute outfits for Hope in tiny baby size, the cutest and softest little polar bear, and a board book. 'And we need to take something for Freya, too.'

'Not flowers or balloons,' Josh said. 'They're the first things that get banned as part of virus control regulations.'

'Nice smellies, then,' Amy said, and dragged him off to a small shop that specialised in cruelty-free beauty products. 'They're really popular with her year group,' Amy explained, when Josh looked mystified.

'You really do notice things, don't you?' he asked.

'I'm supposed to notice things. I'm a form tutor. And I missed Freya's pregnancy completely,' Amy said, 'so I let her down.'

He gave her a hug. 'I don't think you're the one who let her down, honey.'

She bought wrapping paper, tape, ribbon and a 'congratulations on your baby girl' card, and they stopped for a very brief coffee so Amy could wrap the presents.

'How do you do that?' Josh asked when he saw the beautifully wrapped parcels and curled ribbons. 'I wrap something and—well, I think a five-year-old could do a better job than I do.'

'It's all about angles,' she said.

'Maths teacher stuff.' He rolled his eyes.

'You got it.' She winked at him. 'But, given that you have to stitch people up without leaving scars, surely you can wrap things?'

'Wrapping,' he said, 'is way harder than suturing. Trust me on that.' He grinned. 'Let's go and see the girls.'

They learned from the midwife at the reception desk that Freya was still in room six, and Josh rapped softly on the door. 'Freya? Hello? Can we come in?'

'Josh! You said you'd come back,' she said, looking pleased to see him.

'I promised you a sketch. And I'm off duty today, so I thought now would work nicely.'

'It's so nice to see you. Thank you ever so much. It was getting a bit—well…'

'Boring, on your own?' he asked.

'A bit.' She beamed at him. 'Hope, we've got a visitor.' But then she bit her lip when she saw Amy walk into the room behind Josh. 'Oh—Miss Howes! I'm so sorry for what I did.'

'We're out of school, so you can call me Amy, and there's absolutely no need for you to apologise because you've really had a hard time,' Amy said, and gave the girl a hug. 'How are you doing?'

'I'm getting better.' A tear slid down Freya's face. 'But I ruined your Christmas.'

'No, you fixed it,' Amy said, 'because I was meant to be spending it in Edinburgh with my oldest friends—but they got the flu, so I was going to be all alone and miserable at home. Instead, I got to spend Christmas with Josh and Hope.'

'That's what he said when he came yesterday.'

Amy smiled. 'I promise we didn't confer before-hand—and how's your gorgeous baby?'

Freya indicated the crib to the side of the bed. 'She's asleep right now. Thank you for looking after her.'

'I enjoyed it,' Amy said. 'Though it was a bit of a steep learning curve—I'm more used to dealing with teenagers.' She paused and took Freya's hand. 'You could've come to talk to me, Freya, and you still can. Any time. And if you want to come back to school and do your exams, we can support you and make sure you have everything you need.'

'Really?'

'Really,' Amy said firmly.

Another tear slid down Freya's cheek. 'I wish my mum would be like you.'

'She's not been to see you yet?' Amy asked.

Freya shook her head. 'And I'm kind of glad, be-cause I don't want to see her.'

'But you've just had a baby—surely you want your mum.'

Freya nodded, and this time she burst into tears.

Amy held her until she stopped crying.

'I don't want to give Hope away,' Freya said, 'but she'll make me. And there's nothing I can do, because who's going to let a fifteen-year-old with a baby live with them?'

Amy glanced at Josh. She could think of a solution that might work for all of them. But she couldn't say anything to Freya until she'd discussed it with Josh. Saying that you'd consider fostering someone and ac-tually doing it were two very different things.

'Things will get better with your mum,' Amy said. 'Sometimes when you're very lonely you make wrong decisions.'

Josh looked worried, as if he thought that was a coded message to him—that she'd been lonely and agreeing to a relationship with him had been a wrong decision. She caught his eye and gave the tiniest shake of her head to reassure him, then blew him a secret kiss, and saw the tension in his shoulders relax again.

'Maybe giving each other a bit of space will help your mum make a different decision,' Amy said gently.

'She'll still choose him over me.'

Amy thought that was probably true, but it wouldn't help anything to agree with Freya right at that moment. 'It's always difficult to second-guess what someone else is going to do and right now I think you need to concentrate on yourself and the baby,' she said. 'Josh tells me you had an infection.'

Freya nodded. 'They're giving me antibiotics. And I feel a bit better than I did.'

'That's good,' Amy said.

'And we brought you both a little something,' Josh said, handing Freya the parcels and the card.

Freya opened the parcel with the sleep suits and the tiny dungarees and sweater. 'Oh, they're gorgeous,' she said. 'Look, Hope. Your first present.' She was in tears again by the time she'd unwrapped the polar bear, and sobbing openly when she opened the gift for her.

'Hey.' This time Josh was the one to give her a hug.

'It's just…'

'It's all a bit overwhelming,' Josh said, 'and you've just had a baby. Do you want me to leave the sketch until another day?'

'When my face isn't all blotchy and stuff? Yes, please.' Freya looked forlorn. 'Or is that being vain and greedy?'

'Of course it's not,' Josh reassured her.

Amy took her hand and squeezed it. 'Has Alice come to visit you yet?'

'No, even though I texted her to let her know I'm here.' Freya bit her lip. 'She probably thinks I don't want to see her because she told her mum everything when she promised me she'd keep it secret.'

'I wouldn't normally act as a go-between,' Amy said, 'but I think this is a special case. Do you want me to have a word with her?'

'Would you?'

'Of course I will.' Amy smiled at her. 'Tell you what—how about I take a photo of you and Hope on my phone to show her?'

'Even though my face is all blotchy?'

'Sweetie, you look just fine. And it's not going to be plastered all over social media, I promise. It's just so I can show Alice.'

Freya brightened, and Amy took the photograph.

She and Josh had a brief cuddle with the baby. 'We'd better let you get some rest,' Amy said, 'but we can come back and see you tomorrow, if you like?'

Freya's eyes filled with tears again, and she scrubbed them away. 'Sorry. I'm being pathetic. That'd be really nice. We'd like that, wouldn't we, Hope?'

The baby gurgled, as if in agreement.

Amy and Josh went from the hospital to Alice's house. Alice's mother opened the door to them. 'Oh, Miss Howes! Is there…?'

Amy smiled at her. 'I just wanted to say thank you for persuading Alice to talk to Jane Richards about Freya. This is my friend, Josh Farnham. And I wondered if we could see Alice for about two minutes?'

'Yes, that's fine. Come in.'

Alice's mother called the teenager down from her room.

'Miss Howes!' Alice stopped dead in the doorway.

'Hello, Alice. This is my friend, Josh,' Amy introduced him swiftly. 'We came to show you something.' Amy opened the photograph on her phone and handed it to Alice.

'Oh—Freya and her baby! But she's so tiny!' Alice said on seeing the baby. 'But how did you...?'

'Freya left the baby on our doorstep on Christmas Eve,' Amy said. 'We kind of worked out that Freya was the mum—but, without your help in confirming that so we could help her, Freya would be very ill right now. So well done for being so brave.'

'But isn't Freya angry with me for telling?' Alice asked, looking worried. 'I mean, she hasn't texted me or anything, and she hasn't been on any of the usual social media. I thought her mum had confiscated her phone and laptop but, after Miss Richards talked to me about the baby, I thought maybe Freya just didn't want to speak to me.'

'I think she's relieved you did tell, actually. She said she'd texted you to say she was in hospital,' Josh said.

'Oh, no! But I didn't get her text,' Alice said biting her lip.

'Josh and I have been her only visitors. She'd really love it if you came to see her,' Amy said gently.

'I think she's worried that you don't want anything to do with her any more.'

'But that's daft. She's my best friend. Of course I want to see her—and the baby. Can we, Mum?' Alice asked.

Alice's mum nodded. 'Of course. We'll go and buy her something nice for the baby too—I assume she's keeping the baby, Miss Howes?'

'She wants to, yes. Her little girl's called Hope.'

'That's nice.'

Amy smiled in agreement, 'And, Alice, I hope you know you can always talk to me in confidence,' she said. 'Sometimes I might have to act on what you tell me—like the social worker did, to keep Freya safe—but that's why I'm your form tutor. I'm there if you need me.'

Alice blushed, clearly not quite sure what to say. 'Thank you.'

'Anyway—we'd better go,' Amy said. 'But thanks for all your help. You did the right thing.'

Alice's mum showed them out. 'I feel better knowing there's someone like you at school keeping an eye out for the kids,' she said.

'Me? I'm just ordinary,' Amy said.

And Josh thought, no, you're not ordinary. You're really special.

Once they'd left Alice's house, Josh steered them towards the nearest coffee shop. 'I think we need to talk,' he said.

'Agreed.'

He ordered them both coffee and found a quiet table. 'Poor Freya's really been through the mill.'

'And she clearly doesn't want to go back to her

mum's, as you said yesterday. She wants to keep the baby. And she thinks she's not going to be able to do that.'

'She told me yesterday she was scared she'd end up in a children's home and everyone there would despise her.'

'Poor kid.' Amy winced. 'You know what you were saying about considering fostering?'

'Yes.' Even though he knew he was probably rushing it, Josh was pretty sure that Amy was thinking along exactly the same lines as he was. 'I think we've just found two kids who need us to be their family.'

'It's a lot to ask, Josh. Teenagers aren't easy, and neither are babies. Plus this thing between you and me—this is all really new.'

He took her hand. 'But it's also really *right*. With you, I feel as if I've found the place where I fit.'

'Me, too.' She tightened her fingers round his. 'There are probably regulations against me fostering her because I'm her form tutor.'

'There's probably a way to cut through the red tape. And we know someone who'll help,' Josh pointed out. 'Because this is a solution where we're all going to win. We all get a family. You're right in that it's not going to be plain sailing, but we can work on it together.' He paused. 'So. Your flat or mine?'

'That's a problem. Both our flats have only one bedroom, and we're going to need at least two—if not three,' Amy said.

'So either we rent out our flats and then take out a lease on a bigger place,' he said. 'Or we could sell the flats, pool our resources and buy a bigger place together.'

She took a sip of coffee. 'You know, a week ago, I was on my own and focused on my career. If someone had told me that just one week later I'd find someone who feels like my missing half and we'd be talking about house-hunting together, I would never have believed them.'

'Yeah, it's fast. Scarily fast.' He took a deep breath. 'And it was fast for me with Kelly, too, and you know that went wrong, so I'm not surprised you're having doubts. Though, just so you know, I'm not having doubts.'

'I'm not having doubts, either. Doing things fast went wrong for you last time; but doing things slowly went wrong for me the last two times. So maybe we just need to forget about the past. We're both older and wiser, and we're not going to repeat our mistakes,' she said. 'We're looking to the future. Together.'

'You, me, and a ready-made family of a teen and a baby. Works for me,' he said. 'It's not going to be perfect, and we're going to have downs as well as ups, but I'm sure this is the right thing.'

'Me, too,' Amy agreed.

'Now we just need to sort out the red tape.'

'Do you want to call Jane, or shall I?' Amy asked.

'We'll do it together,' he said. 'Just as we're going to tackle everything else.'

She took out her phone, switching it to speaker mode so Josh could hear as well, and called Jane.

'Jane? It's Amy and Josh. We were wondering—can we see you today, please?'

'Sorry, no can do. I'm afraid I'm stacked up with meetings,' Jane said.

'But you have to have a lunch break, right?' Josh asked.

'Right.' Jane sounded wary.

'If we meet you with sandwiches and coffee,' Josh said, 'can we steal the ten minutes it would've taken you to queue up to get your coffee?'

Jane gave a wry laugh. 'You obviously both really want to talk to me.'

'We do,' they said in unison.

'All right. One o'clock in the picnic bit in the park opposite my office—not because I'm trying to wriggle out of anything but, if I meet you in the office, someone's bound to drag me off into another meeting,' she said.

'The park's perfect,' Amy said.

She gave them the details; at one o'clock, Josh and Amy were waiting in the park with sandwiches, cake and coffee.

Five minutes later, Jane rushed over. 'Sorry. I couldn't get off the phone.' Her eyes widened at the array of food. 'Wow. I should let you hijack my lunch break more often.'

'We forgot to ask you what you like, so there's a variety,' Josh said.

'Fabulous. Thank you. Right. So what do you want to talk to me about?' she asked, gratefully accepting the paper cup of coffee that Amy handed to her.

'We've been to see Freya,' Amy said.

'Which is *not* what I would've advised,' Jane said.

Josh spread his hands. 'We happened to be in the area.'

Jane scoffed. 'Right.'

'She told us she doesn't want to go back to live with her mum,' Amy said.

'I don't particularly want her doing that, either,' Jane said grimly.

'But she's worried about who's going to take in a fifteen-year-old with a baby,' Josh said.

'And we have a solution,' Amy added with a smile. 'Something that means everyone wins.'

'I have no idea how you get accepted as a foster parent,' Josh said, 'but we were hoping you'd know how to cut through all the red tape and fast-track it for us.'

Jane blinked. 'Hang on. Are you telling me that you'd be prepared to foster both Freya and Hope?'

'Together,' Amy said. 'Yes.'

'But...' Jane looked confused. 'Last week, when I first met you and you agreed to look after Hope, you said you were just neighbours and barely knew each other.'

'That,' Josh said, 'was before the Christmas that changed everything. We want to be a family. And we want Freya and Hope included in that family.'

'Which is a really good start. Though you'll both have to go through an assessment process,' Jane said, 'and, if you pass—though I'm pretty sure you will—then you'll need training.'

'That's fine. School holidays won't be a problem,' Amy said, 'given that I'm a teacher.'

'You'll need a spare room,' Jane warned. 'And, with you both being in separate flats, probably one of you will have to be named as the main foster carer.'

'We've already talked about that,' Josh said, 'and we plan to go house-hunting for a place big enough for all of us.'

'It's a new year and new beginning,' Amy said. 'For all of us.'

'Then in that case,' Jane said, 'I'll do everything I can to help make this work.'

Amy and Josh lifted their paper cups of coffee in a toast. 'We'll drink to that. Our new family.'

EPILOGUE

A year later—Christmas Eve

'You look amazing,' Amy's father, George, said outside the hospital chapel.

'Utterly gorgeous.' Amy's mother, Patricia, tweaked Amy's headdress and veil. 'And so do you two,' she added to Freya, who was carrying Hope in one arm and a bouquet in her free hand. 'My three girls. Look at you. And our little Hope looks so cute in that dress.'

Amy blinked back the tears. Her parents had taken Freya and Hope straight to their hearts and insisted that they were part of the family, even before the fostering had become official.

'We need a picture, George,' Patricia said.

'All four of you together. *My* girls,' he added proudly.

They posed for the photograph, and then Patricia went to sit in the front row at the chapel.

'Ready for this?' George asked softly.

'Absolutely ready,' Amy said. 'How about you, Freya?'

'Bring it on,' the teenager said with a smile.

* * *

Josh looked back down the aisle. The hospital chapel was packed with their family and friends; and his brother was standing beside him as his best man. Since Amy had been in his life, his relationship with his family had been a lot less prickly; although his family had been unnerved at first by his unconventional ready-made family, Amy had made them see that it worked and Josh was actually happy.

Amy's brother Scott was sitting at the piano; when Patricia sat down in the front row of the chapel, Scott took his cue to begin playing the largo from 'Winter' from Vivaldi's *Four Seasons*.

And then the door opened and Amy walked down the aisle towards him on her father's arm. Her short veil was held in place by a narrow crown of deep red roses, to match the ones in her bouquet, and she wore a very simple cream ankle-length dress. Behind them walked Freya as the bridesmaid, wearing a dark red version of Amy's dress, holding Hope in her arms, also wearing a dark red version of Amy's dress, but with the addition of a cream fluffy bolero to keep her warm.

My family, Josh thought.

And from today it would be that little bit more official, with Amy becoming Mrs Farnham.

Christmas Eve was the perfect day for their wedding day. A year since they'd first got to know each other properly. The anniversary of the beginning of the happiest days of their lives—and it would only get better.

'I love you, Mrs-Farnham-to-be,' he mouthed as Amy joined him at the altar.

'I love you, too,' she mouthed back.

They'd chosen to sing carols rather than hymns, picking the happiest ones that everyone knew—'Silent Night', 'Hark the Herald Angels Sing' and 'O Little Town of Bethlehem'.

And, after the ceremony, everyone in the congregation sang 'All You Need Is Love', accompanied by Scott on the piano, as Amy and Josh walked down the aisle for the first time as a married couple.

They'd booked the reception at the hotel across the road from the hospital, with a simple sit-down meal for their family and closest friends; but they'd also invited Jane the social worker and Freya's mum.

After the meal, Amy's father stood up. 'I'd like to thank everyone for coming today. Patricia and I are absolutely delighted to welcome Josh into our family—he's a lovely man, a great doctor and a fantastic artist. But, most of all, he makes my daughter happy, and as parents that's all that Patricia and I want. And I'm also delighted that we have Freya and Hope as well. So I'd like everyone to raise their glasses: I give you Josh, Amy, Freya and Hope.'

Once everyone had echoed the toast, Josh stood up. 'I'd like to thank George, Patricia, Scott and Rae for making me feel like part of their family from the first moment they met me. Today's a special day for me—it's the first Christmas Eve since my graduation where I haven't been on duty in the Emergency Department. That means this is my first real family Christmas, and I'm loving every second of it so far. Today's the first anniversary of the beginning of the happiest time in my life. So I'd like you to raise a glass to my beautiful bride, Amy, who's made me the happiest man alive, and to our beautiful bridesmaid and ring-bearer, Freya and Hope, who bring joy to our lives every day.'

'Amy, Freya and Hope,' everyone chorused.

Josh's brother Stuart stood up next. 'It's really good to see my brother so happy. And I couldn't be more thrilled to welcome Amy, Freya and Hope to our family. Because of them, my son and my two nieces are getting to see much more of their uncle. They're living proof that no matter how unconventional a family might seem, if they love each other, it'll all work out.' He smiled. 'I have a feeling the rest of the speeches aren't going to be very conventional, either. So, instead of telling you stories about Josh, I'm going to hand you over to his colleagues and Amy's to tell you what their life is like.'

The head of the music department at Amy's school stood up. 'Most of the time I get my classes to sing this as a cumulative song, but today we're doing just the last verse for you, because we'd like you to know what Christmas Eve is usually like for a maths teacher and an emergency department doctor.'

Josh took Amy's hand and squeezed it.

'Did you know about this?' she asked.

He grinned. 'Just a little bit.'

The head of music was joined by five more of Amy's colleagues and six of Josh's. Together, they sang the first line: 'On the twelfth day of Christmas, for Josh and Amy...'

Then each sang a line in turn and sat down again.

Twelve lesson-plannings,
Eleven past papers,
Ten simultaneous equations,

Nine books to mark,
Eight probabilities,
Seven bits of algebra,
Six Colles' fractures,
Five turkey carvers!
Four black eyes,
Three throwing up,
Two broken ankles,
And a bead up a toddler's nose.

Everyone applauded, and the singers all stood up again to take a bow.

Then it was Amy's turn to speak. 'I'd like to thank the Farnhams for taking us all to their hearts and making us part of their family. Thank you very much to our colleagues for their revue—absolutely spot on. And I'm afraid there's a little bit more singing now, because it's a very special person's first birthday. Without her, Josh and I might never have met properly, so please join with us in singing a very special song for Hope.'

At her signal, one of the waitresses brought out a chocolate cake in the shape of a figure one, with a single candle, and placed it on the table in front of Freya and the toddler.

Everyone sang happy birthday to Hope; Freya helped her daughter blow out the candle. When everyone cheered, Hope clapped her hands and looked thoroughly pleased with herself.

Then Freya stood up. 'I know it's not usual for the bridesmaid to make a speech, and I'm not very good at talking in public, but there's something I really want to say. Last Christmas was the worst of my life, and...' She paused, her face turning bright red, and then took a deep breath. 'And I thought I'd never see my baby again. This Christmas, life couldn't be any better. I'm thrilled to be celebrating Josh and Amy getting married, as well as Hope's first birthday. Amy's taught me so much and Josh has inspired me to become a nurse. They've both been really fantastic foster parents—and they've helped make things better with my mum, too. And Mum helped me to make something special for them.'

Freya's mother quietly took a parcel from beneath the table and handed it to Freya, who walked over to Amy and Josh and hugged them both before giving the parcel to them.

Together, they opened it to find the most beautiful frame containing a photograph of the four of them from the summer, on their first day in their new house.

Everyone clapped; Freya's face turned bright red again and she sat down again very quickly.

Josh and Amy stood up together, then. 'Thank you, Freya. It's the perfect present,' Josh said.

'And we're so glad that everyone's here today to share our special day with us,' Amy added.

'We'll cut the cake in a second,' Josh said.

'But before we start the dancing we want everyone to just chill out, relax and have a good time,' Amy finished. 'Because we really want to come and say hello to everyone and have a chat. Just have a drink while you're waiting for cake.'

Everyone clapped, and they posed for photographs before they cut the cake.

Freya's mum hugged both of them when they got to her. 'Thank you both so much. It's because of you that I'm starting to rebuild my relationship with Freya. I know it's not going to be easy, but your support means a lot to both of us. Thank you for doing for her what I was...' She grimaced. 'Well, too stupid to see. And I still can't believe you actually invited me to your wedding.'

'You're Freya's mum. That makes you part of our family,' Amy said, and hugged her.

'Everyone makes mistakes,' Josh said quietly, 'and everyone deserves a second chance. I'm really glad you came, because I think you need to be here on your granddaughter's first birthday—and it means a lot to Freya and Hope that you're here.'

Freya's mum swallowed hard. 'Thank you.'

Everyone seemed to be happy for them, Amy thought. And Jane also greeted them both with a hug. 'You two are my big success story,' she said. 'I remember last Christmas. And seeing you with Freya and Hope—well, you really make me feel my job's worthwhile. On the days when everything's going wrong, I think of you two and it makes everything a lot better.'

When they'd finally managed to have a word with everyone and were back in their seats at the top table, Josh's brother Stuart stood up.

'Ladies and gentlemen—it's time for the first dance,' he said. 'I have it on very reliable information that our Josh sings this to stop babies crying, and it actually works, so see me later if you want to hire him.'

Everyone laughed.

'But, seriously, this is the perfect song for the perfect couple at a perfect Christmas wedding. I give you Josh and Amy,' he said, and the DJ began to play 'All I Want for Christmas is You'.

Josh took his bride in his arms and danced her round

the floor. 'I love you,' he said, 'and this is the best Christmas ever.'

'I love you, too,' Amy said. 'And you're right. Today, I have everything I've ever wanted: you and our new family.'

'You and our new family,' he echoed, and kissed her.

* * * * *

MILLS & BOON®
Hardback – December 2016

ROMANCE

A Di Sione for the Greek's Pleasure	Kate Hewitt
The Prince's Pregnant Mistress	Maisey Yates
The Greek's Christmas Bride	Lynne Graham
The Guardian's Virgin Ward	Caitlin Crews
A Royal Vow of Convenience	Sharon Kendrick
The Desert King's Secret Heir	Annie West
Married for the Sheikh's Duty	Tara Pammi
Surrendering to the Vengeful Italian	Angela Bissell
Winter Wedding for the Prince	Barbara Wallace
Christmas in the Boss's Castle	Scarlet Wilson
Her Festive Doorstep Baby	Kate Hardy
Holiday with the Mystery Italian	Ellie Darkins
White Christmas for the Single Mum	Susanne Hampton
A Royal Baby for Christmas	Scarlet Wilson
Playboy on Her Christmas List	Carol Marinelli
The Army Doc's Baby Bombshell	Sue MacKay
The Doctor's Sleigh Bell Proposal	Susan Carlisle
The Baby Proposal	Andrea Laurence
Maid Under the Mistletoe	Maureen Child

MILLS & BOON®
Large Print – December 2016

ROMANCE

The Di Sione Secret Baby	Maya Blake
Carides's Forgotten Wife	Maisey Yates
The Playboy's Ruthless Pursuit	Miranda Lee
His Mistress for a Week	Melanie Milburne
Crowned for the Prince's Heir	Sharon Kendrick
In the Sheikh's Service	Susan Stephens
Marrying Her Royal Enemy	Jennifer Hayward
An Unlikely Bride for the Billionaire	Michelle Douglas
Falling for the Secret Millionaire	Kate Hardy
The Forbidden Prince	Alison Roberts
The Best Man's Guarded Heart	Katrina Cudmore

HISTORICAL

Sheikh's Mail-Order Bride	Marguerite Kaye
Miss Marianne's Disgrace	Georgie Lee
Her Enemy at the Altar	Virginia Heath
Enslaved by the Desert Trader	Greta Gilbert
Royalist on the Run	Helen Dickson

MEDICAL

The Prince and the Midwife	Robin Gianna
His Pregnant Sleeping Beauty	Lynne Marshall
One Night, Twin Consequences	Annie O'Neil
Twin Surprise for the Single Doc	Susanne Hampton
The Doctor's Forbidden Fling	Karin Baine
The Army Doc's Secret Wife	Charlotte Hawkes

MILLS & BOON®
Hardback – January 2017

ROMANCE

A Deal for the Di Sione Ring	Jennifer Hayward
The Italian's Pregnant Virgin	Maisey Yates
A Dangerous Taste of Passion	Anne Mather
Bought to Carry His Heir	Jane Porter
Married for the Greek's Convenience	Michelle Smart
Bound by His Desert Diamond	Andie Brock
A Child Claimed by Gold	Rachael Thomas
Defying Her Billionaire Protector	Angela Bissell
Her New Year Baby Secret	Jessica Gilmore
Slow Dance with the Best Man	Sophie Pembroke
The Prince's Convenient Proposal	Barbara Hannay
The Tycoon's Reluctant Cinderella	Therese Beharrie
Falling for Her Wounded Hero	Marion Lennox
The Surgeon's Baby Surprise	Charlotte Hawkes
Santiago's Convenient Fiancée	Annie O'Neil
Alejandro's Sexy Secret	Amy Ruttan
The Doctor's Diamond Proposal	Annie Claydon
Weekend with the Best Man	Leah Martyn
One Baby, Two Secrets	Barbara Dunlop
The Tycoon's Secret Child	Maureen Child

MILLS & BOON®
Large Print – January 2017

ROMANCE

To Blackmail a Di Sione	Rachael Thomas
A Ring for Vincenzo's Heir	Jennie Lucas
Demetriou Demands His Child	Kate Hewitt
Trapped by Vialli's Vows	Chantelle Shaw
The Sheikh's Baby Scandal	Carol Marinelli
Defying the Billionaire's Command	Michelle Conder
The Secret Beneath the Veil	Dani Collins
Stepping into the Prince's World	Marion Lennox
Unveiling the Bridesmaid	Jessica Gilmore
The CEO's Surprise Family	Teresa Carpenter
The Billionaire from Her Past	Leah Ashton

HISTORICAL

Stolen Encounters with the Duchess	Julia Justiss
The Cinderella Governess	Georgie Lee
The Reluctant Viscount	Lara Temple
Taming the Tempestuous Tudor	Juliet Landon
Silk, Swords and Surrender	Jeannie Lin

MEDICAL

Taming Hollywood's Ultimate Playboy	Amalie Berlin
Winning Back His Doctor Bride	Tina Beckett
White Wedding for a Southern Belle	Susan Carlisle
Wedding Date with the Army Doc	Lynne Marshall
Capturing the Single Dad's Heart	Kate Hardy
Doctor, Mummy... Wife?	Dianne Drake

MILLS & BOON®

Why shop at millsandboon.co.uk?

Each year, thousands of romance readers find their perfect read at millsandboon.co.uk. That's because we're passionate about bringing you the very best romantic fiction. Here are some of the advantages of shopping at www.millsandboon.co.uk:

* **Get new books first**—you'll be able to buy your favourite books one month before they hit the shops

* **Get exclusive discounts**—you'll also be able to buy our specially created monthly collections, with up to 50% off the RRP

* **Find your favourite authors**—latest news, interviews and new releases for all your favourite authors and series on our website, plus ideas for what to try next

* **Join in**—once you've bought your favourite books, don't forget to register with us to rate, review and join in the discussions

Visit **www.millsandboon.co.uk**
for all this and more today!